SECRET

BLACK HOODS MC#2

Dark Secret © 2020 Avelyn Paige & Geri Glenn

Dark Secret

Years ago Shelby Dawson fled, with nothing but a broken heart and a baby on the way. She never expected to see him again. She sure as hell never wanted to need him.

Until her daughter meets the wrong man online. Until her daughter is taken.

When Shelby shows up at the clubhouse, drenched in rain and crying over her missing daughter, he wants to hurt her like she'd hurt him.

But when he discovers the missing daughter is his, he'll rain down hell on whoever took her, and he might just find redemption in the process.

To Ellen B.

It's readers like you that gave us purpose.

Rest easy, special lady.

Chapter 1

Shelby

Thirteen Years Ago

PREGNANT.

That's what the doctor had told me with her disapproving eyes while handing me a pamphlet on my options when finding oneself in this exact situation.

Funny how that single word can change every plan you've made for your future. Suddenly, you and your wants don't matter as much as you thought they did, and your boyfriend isn't your whole world anymore. The only thing that matters is the tiny little being, protected and warm, deep inside your womb. That being becomes your everything.

I swipe another brushstroke of blush across my

cheekbone, staring into the eyes of the girl in the mirror before me. *Is she really ready to be a mother?*

Short and curvy, with fingernails chewed down to the quick. A snub little nose I've hated for every single one of my eighteen years on this earth. Too much eye shadow. Too much mascara. Hair cut short and spiky, with pink locks scattered throughout the blonde strands.

That's just what shows on the outside. There's more to me than all of that, because the best parts are inside, right?

I'm a bright student, a good daughter, and a hard worker, even if that work is at the Frost-N-Freeze. Work is work.

But what about college? What about Wyatt? We have a plan—a solid one.

In September, I'll attend community college in the next town over to pursue a degree in child care. It's not what I truly want to do, but it's the one course I can afford that will provide me a decent living. Wyatt is being patched into the Black Hoods MC, who are talking about sending him to school to get his degree in computer sciences. We've talked about our future at length. Wyatt has so many plans for us, but would that *us* include a plus one?

Nibbling on my lower lip, I place my hand on my belly. We now have this little peanut to think of, and

Wyatt doesn't even know yet. What's he going to say? Which option of that teen pregnancy pamphlet is he going to want to choose?

"Shelby!" my dad calls from downstairs. "Miss Kasey's here."

"I'll be right down!" I call through the cracked bedroom door. *Shit.* Kasey is going to know something's up the instant she lays eyes on me. But should I tell her?

No, I shouldn't. Not yet. Kasey can't stand Wyatt; she's going to be pissed.

Besides, this news is for Wyatt to hear first, then Kasey. Then—I shudder at the thought—my father. If he hated Wyatt before, knowing I'm having his baby will send him through the roof and straight to the moon.

Flicking my fingers through my hair one last time, I rearrange a few strands to ensure they're standing at a perfect, haphazard angle, snatch my purse off the end of the bed, and make my way down the stairs.

"Hey," I greet Kasey as I press a kiss to my father's cheek, ignoring the burden of my secret when I pull away.

"You girls behave," he asserts from his place in his favorite recliner. "I spent your bail money on a case of beer."

He wouldn't be saying that if he knew where we were going.

Kasey giggles as if she hasn't heard that same joke from my father a thousand times before. "We're always good, Mr. D."

Dad snorts. Taking another swig of his beer, he warns, "Watch it, Miss Kasey. One of these days your pants are gonna catch on fire."

I roll my eyes. "Bye, Daddy."

In true Kasey form, I've barely closed the door to the house before she's on me.

"What's wrong?"

Laughing, I walk over to her rusted Ford Taurus at the curb. "I don't know what you're talking about. What's wrong with you?"

She glares at me over the roof of the car before climbing into the driver's seat. Once we're both inside and buckled in, she pulls out onto the road, heading toward the Black Hoods' clubhouse.

"Don't lie," she retorts.

How does she always know?

"I'm not lying!"

"Shelby Jo Dawson, I've known you since we were four years old. I was there when you got yourself into trouble with Ms. Lester for gluing her stapler to her desk. I was there when Bobby Dixon tried to kiss you on the bleachers at the homecoming game our freshman year. And I was there when Wyatt Hayden finally made a woman out of you—well, not *there*, at *that* moment, but afterward. You know what I mean. Anyway, I know you better than you know yourself. I could tell straight away you have something going on, and I want to know what it is."

Sagging my shoulders, I blurt out, "I'm pregnant." That's it. Two words. Matter-of-fact. But inside, my heart's hammering, watching from the corner of my eye as she processes the news.

She doesn't say anything. Instead, she drives another few minutes and pulls into a parking space at the clubhouse without a word. Turning off the ignition, she drops the keys into her purse and faces me, staring intently. "I got you, girl. Does Wyatt know?"

Shaking my head, a tear escapes, making its way down my cheek.

Taking my hand, she gives it a tight squeeze. "I've got you."

Music blares out of the clubhouse. This is a big night for the club, and an even bigger night for Wyatt. After becoming a prospect at eighteen, he'd worked his ass off for two years to become a member of the Black Hoods MC.

He'd done things he would never tell me about. He'd learned things that were club business only, and I had quickly figured out it wasn't my place to know. It had been a rough two years for the both of us. But tonight, he gets his patch. Tonight, all his hard work and the struggles we have both faced are paying off. His dream is coming true.

"I can't do this," I announce, reaching behind me and grabbing at the seat belt I'd just removed. "I can't tell him. Not tonight. This is his night."

Kasey grabs my hand once more and holds it still. "This *is* his night. And if finding out he's going to be a father with the woman he loves doesn't make it even better for him, he doesn't deserve you or the baby."

God, I hope she's right.

"Get your ass out of this car and go tell that man he's going to be a daddy." She says it with so much enthusiasm, my fear of his disappointment fades a little.

I climb out of the car and move toward the door of the clubhouse. Kasey loops her arm through mine and grins over at a couple of the guys leaning against their motorcycles. The men here love Kasey, but other than being a total flirt, she never gives them the time of day. It drives most of them nuts.

Inside, the air is thick with smoke, and the music thumps so loud, I can't even hear my hammering heart. I scan the room for Wyatt, but he's nowhere to be seen.

"Two"—she glances back at me—"make that one

beer," Kasey tells the prospect tending bar. "And, do you know where Hashtag is?"

Slamming a bottle of beer onto the bar top, he tips his head toward the hallway. "Last I saw him, he was heading back there to check out his new room."

Ah, right. I'd forgotten about that part. All patched members of the Black Hoods are given a room here at the clubhouse to store their shit or crash. Tonight, Wyatt would be given the key to a room of his own.

"You know which one it is?" I shout over the noise as I move in that direction.

Holding up three fingers, he shouts back, "Room 3A!"

Kasey grabs my shoulder and turns me around to face her, urging, "You've got this."

I try not to let fear overwhelm me as I wade through the crowd and into the hallway. Trying to calm my breathing, I walk past a bunch of closed doors until I reach room 3A. Finding it ajar, I take a deep breath before pushing it open.

I've been inside these rooms before, which are all the same, really: a bed, a dresser, and a nightstand. A small en suite bathroom is off to the side, complete with a shower. So, his room is basically what I expected, except for one thing.

I never expected to see Layla and Sasha in his bed —naked.

Sasha, whose back is to me, is riding the man beneath her. I can't see his face, but from his moans, and the way his toes are curled, I'd be wise to assume he's thoroughly enjoying it.

Layla, however, is facing me. She's up near the headboard, her pussy pressed against his face, her hands full of Sasha's tits. When she sees me, she freezes, her eyes wide with shock. Then, curling her lips up in an evil grin, she rocks her hips faster.

She doesn't stop. She doesn't tell Sasha I'm standing here. Instead, she continues to ride Wyatt's face, making a show of how much she's enjoying it.

All of this happens in a matter of seconds. I don't make a sound. They don't hear my heart shatter into a million pieces. They don't hear me sob as I turn and bolt down the hallway.

I knew Wyatt was around women all the time at the club, including Layla, and it's no secret she and I don't get along. Hell, it's been the cause of a lot of our quarrels. But I never believed in a million years he would betray me like this.

"What happened?" Kasey probes, her face twisted in anger and confusion as I approach.

I push past her, rushing toward the door. "I want to get out of here."

"Shelby!" she calls out, scrambling to keep up with me. "Shelby, wait! What's going on?"

Tears pour down my cheeks like a waterfall as I make my way to her car. Pressing my hands against my belly, I think of my tiny peanut, and how Wyatt's betrayed us both.

The locks click when Kasey presses the button and I climb inside, wiping my hot tears on my sleeves.

"What the fuck is going on? What did that asshole do?" she asks as she settles herself behind the wheel.

The pain in my chest has me gasping for breath between sobs. "Just get me out of here, Kase, please?"

When her warm hand lands on mine, I turn and look her in the eyes when she assures, "Shelby, I've got you."

Hashtag

IF YOU HAD ASKED me where I saw myself after graduating high school, I'd never had said being a member of an MC. I was destined for a nine-to-five life. But, when a friend hooked me up with Judge for a job, it all just kind of happened. One little hacking job turned into two, then to prospecting. Now, two years later, I'm a full member.

Fuck, it feels good to finally have my member patch stitched to my cut.

A culmination of two years—two hard fucking years —of grunt work for the members had paid off. If I never see another dirty bike with a bucket and a toothbrush again, I'll die a happy damn man.

The last few years haven't been without personal sacrifices. Shelby, my girlfriend, had been along for the ride. All throughout high school, she was right by my side. When I missed classes to do shit for the club, she helped me catch up on any work I'd missed. When I had to cancel a date at the last minute, she never got upset with me. This woman gave her all to help me succeed. Had it not been for a shared detention period, the two of us may have never met in the first place.

I was the bad boy she couldn't resist, and she was the good girl I corrupted. She grew up surrounded by a big family and old money, whereas I bounced around from foster home to foster home until I turned eighteen. No longer the state's problem, I was out on my ass without a second thought. We're as opposite as you can get, but we work.

When the MC came into my life, I would never have imagined how much it would appeal to me. I wish I could say the same about Shelby, though, as it's always been a struggle for her. How she ended up with a guy like me, I'll never know. But that woman is my fucking everything.

Her sacrifices for me end tonight.

This party isn't just about me—it's about us. I may be a full member, but I plan to make her my old lady in front of the club tonight. More than that, really, but the second half of our night would be away from the eyes of the club. The ring has been burning a hole in my pocket since

I picked it up this morning from the pawnshop. The owner, Bobby, offered to let me do a little side work to pay for it.

"Looks like you've already been celebrating, enjoying your party and what club life has to offer already. I like the enthusiasm." Judge's voice echoes from the doorway of my new room at the clubhouse, his massive arms crossed in front of his equally massive chest. Stepping into the room, he spies the large set of boxes near the desk I'd moved in earlier today. "The fuck is all this?"

"My computer."

His brow arches at my response. "You need all those boxes to do that web shit you do?"

"Can't work my magic on an ancient phone like yours, Judge. How long have you had that thing, anyway? It belongs in a museum."

He pulls out his first-generation iPhone from his back pocket and holds it up to me. "A phone is for calling people. I don't need all those bells and whistles you have on yours. I type in a number, it calls. All a phone should do." If he thinks my secondhand iPhone is high tech, I can't imagine what he'd think of the new top-of-the-line phones on the market now.

"That thing should be a damn doorstop," I tease him.

"Still works, doesn't it?"

"For now. It's one iOS update from crashing."

"I'm going to pretend I understood whatever shit you just said to me." Pocketing his phone, he retrieves something else from his pocket and tosses it to me. They jingle as I catch them in my hand.

I examine the key on the keychain. "What's this?"

"No patch of mine rides a hand-me-down. It's time you have a ride that matches your rank." He smiles at me like a father would smile to his son, pride clear as day on his gray bearded face. "Paying for your tuition this fall is a small drop in the bucket of what this club can give you. This is just a taste, son. You keep it up, there'll be more for you and your girl."

Judge saw my potential after I completed my first job for him a couple years back. I'd always been good with computers, and I'm only going to get better once I start college in the fall: a gift from the club to expand their capabilities. After all the years of my foster parents telling me I was going to end up a drug addict like my mom, the club is giving me an opportunity I could never have afforded on my own, giving Shelby and I a shot at a good start in our lives.

"She's outside if you want to take a look."

He leaves the room, and I follow behind him through the main room of the clubhouse and out the rear entrance. Under the floodlights of the building sits a cherry red 2016 VRSCDX Night Rod Special. It's the exact bike

I've been eyeballing for the better part of the last six months, every time one of the members sends me to the local Harley dealership for parts. How in the hell did they know I'd been looking at her?

"You've got to be shitting me, Judge. No fucking way."

"You just gonna stand there, or you gonna check out your new ride?" Twat Knot yells out from one of the patio chairs around the fire pit that just yesterday, I power washed for my own damn party. His parting gift as my mentor. *Asshat*. A few of the other club guys sit around him with some of the club girls in their laps. "If you don't want it, I'll take it off your hands."

"The fuck you will," Judge growls, clapping his large hand over my shoulder. "Go check her out, son."

I stalk over to the beautiful piece of machinery and run my hands over her smooth exterior.

"You're rubbing that bike like you're touching a woman, dude. Get a room," Karma ribs from the peanut gallery. "Your girl's not going to like another woman being in your life."

"Fuck you."

"No thanks, sugar tits. My dance card's full tonight." He gives the perky little blonde sitting on his lap a squeeze, making her squeal. "Where's your lady at, anyway? Figured she'd be riding your cock with all these girls around, staking her claim."

"She'll be here any minute." Shelby had called earlier to say she was going to be a little late, and that she'd meet me here at the party. She usually rides my ass about arriving early to shit like this, but maybe her dad's giving her shit over coming out to the clubhouse again. I've been telling her to just let me talk to him, but she won't allow it. I know the son of a bitch hates me, but if she says yes tonight, he's going to have to get used to seeing me around. Normally, I'd be annoyed, but it gave me more time to get shit done in my new room.

"She bringing that hot friend of hers? The one with the small rack and great personality?" The bastard winks at me and starts laughing. Twat Knot has an eye for the ladies, and he's been chasing after Kasey since the first time she came to one of our parties. The one voted most likely to be Texas's Biggest Queen Bitch. Shelby's best friend. My adversary. Any time Shelby gets into trouble, Kasey is always by her side. She's a bad influence on her, and that's saying something coming from her outlaw biker boyfriend. Kasey is the last person I want around my girl, and has been the reason for several of our most recent fights.

I shoot him the middle finger. "Fuck you, dickhead."

If I didn't have to take Kasey as a package deal, I'd

have put a stop to her attending the club's parties long ago. We don't need that kind of evil polluting the air. How Shelby can stand to be around her is lost on me, because two seconds into being in her presence, I want to gouge out my eyes.

"I thought she'd be the first person you'd want at your party."

"Let me repeat myself: Fuck you, dickhead."

"It's cute when you get your feathers all ruffled up like that."

"Have you seen my girl or not?"

"Maybe you missed her, being holed up in your room all night. You're missing out on all the fun, kid, seeing as your patch party only happens once. You should be out sampling the buffet." He runs his finger down the cleavage of one of the hang-arounds.

"Looks like that one's been sampled enough by the looks of it." The girl on his lap sneers at me.

Sneering back, I peer down at my phone. She's more than twenty minutes later than when she told me she'd be here. Definitely not like my girl. I pocket the keys to my new ride and head back inside, thinking maybe I'd passed her when Judge and I had walked out. The party has been raging for hours. She might have snuck in and not made it back to meet me in my room like we'd talked about earlier.

I scan the clubhouse, but see no sign of her.

Swiping my finger across the screen, I pull up my contacts and call her number. It rings twice and goes to her voicemail.

"The fuck?" I mumble, trying again. This time, it goes straight to voicemail. I try a third time and get the same thing. Without a second thought, I bolt from the clubhouse and straight to my bike.

"Where's the fire, Hash?" GP yells out as I pass by, but I don't acknowledge him, my focus solely on Shelby. She never ignores my calls, not even when she's pissed at me. I need to find her and figure out why she's ducking me. With a flick of the ignition, my bike roars to life between my legs.

I check my phone one more time before taking off. Nothing. No return calls. No texts. No alerts. The cameras I have set up around the apartment the club had been letting me use hadn't sent any notifications to my phone all afternoon. If she's there, the chance of her not tripping the cameras is slim. The club life's dangerous, and having eyes on her and our soon-to-be temporary home are priority to me when we're out handling club business. Where the fuck could she be? I audibly growl when *her* name pops into my head.

Fucking Kasey. Pounding in her number, she picks up on the second ring, the road noise filling the receiver.

"Where's Shelby?" I demand harshly. "I know she's with you."

"She's not your problem anymore, asshole."

"The hell she isn't."

"Why would she want to be with someone like you? Lose our numbers, prick." The line goes dead.

Fucking bitch. She's done something. Shelby wouldn't run out on me like this. I have to find her.

Popping the kickstand, I peel out of the parking lot, swerving in and out of traffic until her apartment building comes into view. I don't even bother trying to find a parking spot, pulling straight up into a loading area near the front entrance of the building. I look around the lot and see Kasey's piece of shit Taurus isn't in her usual spot. Not a good sign. Taking the steps to her place two at a time, I reach the door and pound the fuck out of it.

"Shelby?" I yell. "Darlin', you in there?" Silence. I lean my forehead against the door as I continue to pound on it. "Come on, baby, answer the door."

Think. Where else could she be? Outside of Kasey and I, she doesn't really roll in any other social circles, which is partly my fault. Her dad and stepmom hate my association with the club, and as her dad has put it more times than I can count: I'm putting his little girl in danger. Let's just say that anytime she wants to spend time with me, she has to come up with an excuse to leave the house. It hasn't been easy.

"Fuck!" I scream, punching my fist against the door, leaving a dent in the gray metal. Heading back down to my bike, I fire her up and head to the one place I never wanted to cross the threshold of again—her dad's.

After about a fifteen-minute drive, I arrive at one of the largest homes on the block, nestled into an old money neighborhood on the city's northeast side. Driving right through the open metal gate, I ride straight for the front entrance where her father stands staunchly on the large front porch, his arms folded across his chest. The security system I helped to install for him is doing its job a little too well for my liking.

"Get off my property, boy! You're trespassing!" he shouts, his thick Southern accent biting out every word.

Dismounting my bike, I stalk toward him, every muscle in my body coiled with tension. "Where is she?"

"She's gone."

His words hit me like a freight train. "What do you mean she's gone?"

Charging down the steps, he stops a few feet away from me in the driveway. "My daughter is no longer your concern."

I snap. Lunging, I grab him by the lapels and draw him closer to me. "You'd like it that way, wouldn't you, asshole? But she loves me. She wouldn't just fucking leave like that. What have you done to her?" I growl. "Tell me where she went."

Shelby's dad shoves me back, hard, and with one swing of his arm, he slams his fist into my jaw. Shocked, I fall back, landing on my ass in the gravel driveway.

"My daughter wants nothing more to do with you. She's finally going to live her life *without* you." His eyes are wide and his chest heaves as he stares me down. "You stay the hell away from her."

"Honey, is everything okay?" Shelby's stepmother, Lorna, calls out to us. Looking up, I see her standing at the edge of the porch, shaking. "Do I need to call the police?"

"Everything's fine, sweetheart. Go on inside. He was just leaving." He smiles back at her with a wave, but she doesn't move. Turning his attention back to me, he kneels down, close to my ear, and whispers, "You step foot on my property again, not even your club will be able to protect you from me."

Without another word, he rights himself, turning his back to me. He trudges back up the steps to his wife and they disappear into their house, dismissing me one final time. Dismissing the life I'd had planned for his daughter, just like she had.

With a hole in my chest where my heart should be, I

pick myself up off the ground and walk to my bike, but not without taking one last look at the house of the girl I love before riding away from the property.

On my trip back to the clubhouse, I think about Shelby and what I could have done wrong. She's been my everything. Even as I was getting my patch this morning, my mind was on her and the commitment I had hoped to make to her tonight. The commitment that's burning a hole in my pocket, nestled inside its velvet box.

Chapter 3

Shelby

Present Day

I SLAM my fist down on the detective's desk, sending office supplies scattering onto the floor. "She's not late! Somebody has taken her!"

Detective Fischer leans back in his seat, scanning the debris left from my outburst. "Miss Dawson, I'm simply trying to look at all available avenues. Most cases of a missing teen is the result of them wanting to spread their wings, stepping out on the rules put in place by their parents. They take off, have some fun, then return home with a hangover and needing to sleep it off."

It's all I can do not to reach across his desk, take his smug face into my hands, and shake some sense into him.

"My daughter is twelve years old. She's not a teenager. She's not 'spreading her wings'." I lean forward, getting in his face, and pin him to his seat with a glare. "I'm telling you, there's something wrong here. Hayden always comes straight to my shop after her day at summer camp."

The detective sighs and removes his glasses, rubbing his eyes with the tips of his fingers. "I'll send word to all the units on patrol, okay? But I don't want you to get your hopes up. Your daughter will likely show up before bedtime tonight."

Panic claws its way up my throat. Hayden has been gone for nearly six hours now, and I've watched enough crime shows to know that the first twenty-four hours are the most critical if you want to find a kidnap victim. I'd come to the police when she didn't show up at my tattoo shop after camp, and hadn't arrived home by eight o'clock. Her friends didn't know where she was, and the camp organizers reported she had been there all day.

Hayden is a reliable kid. She goes to a programming and technology camp for gifted kids she affectionately refers to as "Nerd Camp." She follows the rules. She helps out around my shop. She's my little adult in a child's body, and my gut is telling me everything is far from okay right now.

"Do you have kids, Detective?"

His eyes harden. "No, ma'am, I do not."

"Well, let me educate you on what it's like to be a parent with a missing child you know is in danger, yet some know-it-all detective is telling you she doesn't fit the criteria to take her case seriously." He sits a little straighter as my voice grows colder, my anger rising to the surface.

"Your entire reason for getting up every day is gone. The one person you'd lay down your life for has disappeared, and you're the only one who seems to give a shit. And while your world is spinning out of control, and your child is getting farther and farther out of your reach, you have a detective who thinks he knows her better than you do. He lumps her in with a group of kids who have nothing in common with your child other than their age."

I sit back in my seat, fisting my hands. "My daughter is a computer prodigy. She's been developing games and creating code since she was six years old. She has friends at school, but she spends most of her time doing what she loves—coding. Do you know many computer prodigies who like to party, Detective?"

Fischer sighs. "No, ma'am, I do not."

I clench my teeth together. "Issue an Amber Alert. Track down her now."

Fischer shakes his head slowly from side to side. "I'll

have the active units keep an eye out and send her information to other precincts in the area to do the same. But I will not issue an Amber Alert, not yet, as it's only been a few hours. And besides, we aren't sure yet that Hayden has even been kidnapped. We have no suspect, no proof. Is it possible the child is with her father?"

I gape at him, realizing for the first time since sitting down in his office that he's not going to help me. He's not being cruel, or dumb. He's simply following a set of rules that don't always work, and the result is more and more missing children falling through the cracks, into an abyss of mystery, rarely seen or heard from again.

"Hayden doesn't know her father. He has no reason to contact her."

"I'm going to need his name and contact information to determine that for myself."

A pain unrelated to Hayden's disappearance stabs my already aching heart. "That's not necessary, Detective. He doesn't even know Hayden exists. We haven't spoken since the day I found out I was pregnant with her."

"It's still an avenue to look in—"

"No, it's not," I snap. "He's not the person who took her. You're looking in all the wrong fucking places!"

"Please, calm down, Miss Dawson."

I can't sit here another second; it's not helping find

Hayden. I stand, my head held high, and grab my purse. "I don't care what you do or where you look. Issue an APB, something! I just want you to find my daughter."

I stalk out of the police department, not feeling any more confident than I had when I first went in. The cops here in this little Podunk town don't know what the hell they're doing. Fischer will spin in circles, chasing his tail, looking into all the easy avenues before realizing he actually might have to do a little bit of police work to find my baby girl. I can't let her slip through the cracks like so many other kids I've seen on missing posters.

Is it possible the child is with her father?

The question had been like a shock to my system—a wake-up call. There's no way in hell that Hayden could have connected somehow with Wyatt. And even if they had, Wyatt would never have taken her from me. The man I left in the dust years ago may not even be the same person now. That club changes men in ways I'll never be able to understand, including Wyatt.

But maybe he needs to connect with her. Maybe it's time. I've spent a lot of years trying to keep Wyatt Hayden's face from my thoughts, but having his living, breathing, carbon copy sleeping in the sparkly pink bedroom down the hall for all of these years has made that nearly impossible. Every time she glares at me, it's like he's staring at me through her eyes.

My baby is gone. *Our* baby is gone. And as much as I hate to admit it, he may be the only one who can find her before it's too late.

Chapter 4

Hashtag

IT'S nights like this that make me appreciate not being tied down like some of these fuckers. Just watching them parade around with big ass grins on their faces is enough to make me uneasy. I tried the whole relationship thing once, and it fucking broke me. Nobody's gonna get the chance to put me through that shit again. Settling down? Not happening. I'd rather be alone than go through the hell I've been through. No bitch is worth that much bullshit.

Priest plops down next to me at the bar, ordering a drink from one of the club girls bartending for tonight's festivities. Popping the lid, she slides the bottle over to him.

"Great party," he declares, taking a pull from his beer. "She's good for him—for all of us."

I can only nod in response. Yeah, it worked out for him. Blair's good people. I like her. But sitting here watching the two of them celebrate their love isn't going so well for me tonight. It's not Blair or GP. It's not the other people crowding the clubhouse, having a good time. It's the date—*our* date. Thirteen years ago today, I was a newly patched member with a future full of plans: college, a wife—a family. Only one of those actually got checked off my list, while the other two disappeared that same night without so much as a Dear Wyatt letter to explain why I wasn't enough for her. And the ring I bought her? The one I couldn't force myself to hock all these years later? It stays in my dresser drawer, mocking me each and every morning. A reminder not to trust, but a memento of what it really feels like to love.

"What's up your ass?"

"Nothing," I growl. "Just trying to drink my beer without you ladies spoiling it for me."

Priest glances over at me and shakes his head. "You're not happy for them, are you?"

"Didn't say I wasn't."

Priest takes another swig before slamming down the bottle onto the bar, tossing up his fingers to order another one, while Layla, a long-time club girl, saunters over to me with her tits spilling out of her top. She presses them up against me, and I shove her off.

"Not in the mood, sweetheart."

Her painted face saddens at my dismissal, and even that annoys me.

"Layla, when are you gonna get a clue? The guys around here are gonna keep fuckin' ya, but none of them will ever claim you."

Hurt and anger crease her face, and I can tell instantly that I struck a nerve. "Fuck you, Hashtag. I'd rather fuck a dead Billy goat than be claimed by a stuck-up prick like you."

I grab my dick through my jeans. "Bitch, you've been trying to get in my pants for years. Haven't you figured out yet that I wouldn't touch you if you were the last slut on earth? Go fuck a prospect or something."

Growling, she throws up her middle finger before stomping away in a huff.

Priest shakes his head. "I don't get you, man. All these women around here, and I haven't seen you touch a single one of them. You have something against free pussy?"

Fucking asshole. "Hey, I got a question for you."

"What's that?"

"Does this barstool look like a fucking confessional, prospect?"

Without another word, Priest stalks off, the reminder of his rank like a kick in the nuts. Mission accomplished.

Tonight's the kind of night I just want to sit here at the bar, get drunk, and pass out until tomorrow. I shouldn't even be here, seeing as I'm in no mood for celebrating, but ghosting them like Shelby did to me on such a big night for our club isn't in the cards. I'd be disrespecting both GP and Blair if I hadn't shown up. So, here I sit, wallowing like a fucking asshole in my own personal shit instead of celebrating with my club.

"Hot damn!" Karma yells out from the crowd. "Hey, honey, how about you come and sit on my lap?"

Great. One of the club girls must be putting on a show. Grabbing my beer, I start to turn around when...

What the fuck?

A fucking ghost from my past. One I never expected to walk back into this place so long as my lungs still sucked in air. Shelby fucking Dawson. The woman who broke me.

"Is he here?" her voice calls out over the noise, rocking my fucking world. The beer drops from my hand, shattering to the floor, bringing her attention to me.

Fuck me sideways. Ain't no hiding from her now. *Way to go, asshole. Couldn't just make a quick escape, could you?*

She bolts toward me, fear clear as day on that pretty face I used to call mine all those years ago. The face that fucking bailed without so much as a goddamn word.

Each step she takes closer to my location, my heart thuds inside of my chest. The years have been good to her. Damn good. The girl I knew has grown into a woman, and a smoking hot one at that. Her short, spiky, pink and blonde hair has changed into an even punkier look of bright purple. Every pair of unattached male eyes are on her. Hell, even the ones attached are looking. The beast lying dormant inside of me growls, wanting to re-stake my claim on her and force them to look away. But she's not mine anymore. She'd made that clear enough when she left.

"Wyatt," her silky voice calls out to me. A voice I never thought I'd hear again. A voice that still—after everything—has the power to ruin me.

"So, you do remember my name. Figured you'd forgotten it with the way you left."

Her beautiful eyes soften as a tear slides down her cheek. The pained look tells me all I need to know. She's not here for a reunion, nor to apologize for leaving the way she did. She wants something, and she's desperate enough to come to me after all these years.

Well, she came to the wrong fucking man.

"I need your help."

"I ain't in the helping mood, darlin', not anymore. Go ask someone else," I snarl, stepping around her.

"Please," she pleads. "My daughter's gone."

She has a kid? The fact that she could leave me so easily and have a child with someone else doesn't escape me. It's been years, and her moving on should be a given. So why does that hurt so much? I peek at her left hand. No ring. Commitment still isn't her strong suit, it seems.

"Must get that skill from her mother. You were real good at running away yourself."

"I'm not here to rehash the past, Wyatt. I really need your help." Good. There's nothing for the two of us in the past or in the present. She made damn sure of that thirteen years ago.

"Why should I care about some other man's spawn?"

"Because she's yours."

Those words hit me like an electric shock, straight to the heart. I gape at her, unable to move. "Say that again? I could've sworn you said she was mine. Last time I checked, I didn't see my name listed on a birth certificate anywhere."

"My daughter... she's yours." This time, her voice cracks.

I narrow my eyes and take a step closer. "How do you know she's mine? It's been fucking years, Shelby. For all I know, you're lying to me so I'll help you."

"She's twelve, Wyatt. Do the math."

With a frown, I push past her and pace the floor, ignoring the people around us watching our every move.

If she's really twelve, the timing would be right, but why the hell would I believe her? The woman I knew back then wouldn't have hidden this from me. She knew I wanted kids. A tie to someone by blood, since my own family didn't bother to stick around.

"Please, Wyatt," she sobs. "She's missing. I know something's wrong. Someone's taken her."

The hurt in her voice brings every protective instinct I've ever had for her rising back to the surface. Between the noise, the eyes of everyone looking at us, and this fucking revelation swirling around my head, I can't take it anymore.

Reaching out for her hand, she recoils.

"Jesus, Shelby, I'm not going to fucking bite you. We need to go someplace, away from all this noise, so I can think." I reach out for her again, and this time, she allows me to touch her soft hand. I lead her down the hallway, straight toward the room I keep at the clubhouse. She stops dead the second she sees it, her face sullen and white.

"Come on." Opening the door, I drag her inside, releasing her long enough to shut the door and everyone out. Shelby's eyes dart around the space before focusing back on me. A slight tremor rolls down her body, as if she's afraid of me.

"Start from the beginning."

Shelby

I STAND LIKE A STATUE, unable to move a muscle as I take in the room that changed everything about my life as I knew it. I hadn't spent but a few seconds in here that night all those years ago, but from what I can tell, not much has changed.

Computer parts and cords are scattered across every available surface, with boxes stacked in the corner. The bed is made, but rumpled. *At least it's empty.*

"Shelby," Wyatt calls, snapping me back to the here and now. "Your daughter."

I blink at him. *My daughter.* Him saying those words to me is so strange. But she's not just my daughter; she's his too. *Oh, God.* What was I thinking coming here?

"I'm sorry. I shouldn't have come here," I blurt out, bolting past him toward the door.

When it opens just a fraction, my heart soars with hope. I need to get out of this room, out of this clubhouse. Out of this godawful town. But I only get it open a fraction before it's closed with a thud so loud, it rattles the walls around us.

Wyatt stands behind me, so close, I can feel the heat of his chest against my back, his muscled forearm pressing against the door beside me. "I don't fucking think so, sweet cheeks. I'm done watching the ass end of you running away from me. You came to me, asking for help." His words, whispered against my cheek, sends a shiver down my spine. And just for a moment, I revel in his nearness, my eyes falling closed as he moves even closer.

"Fuck," he snarls, pushing away from me and stalking across to the other side of the room. "What the actual fuck, Shelby? You can't just fucking walk back in here thirteen years later and tell me I have a goddamn kid. You think you can drop an atomic bomb like that and just bolt again?"

I press my back against the door and fight back the tears that are already spilling down my cheeks. "I shouldn't have come to you. I shouldn't be here."

Anger and hatred stare back at me from the same eyes that once looked at me with reverence and admiration. "You heartless bitch," he spits. Those words assault my heart like serrated blades, but I still don't move. "You think long and hard about your next move, Shelby. If what you say is true, and that you've been keeping my kid from me all these years, we'll deal with that. But if it's also true this kid is missing, we need to move, and we need to move fast. So, pull your fucking head out of your ass and fill me in so I can find my fucking daughter."

I gape at him before finally dashing away my tears on the backs of my trembling hands. Reaching into my purse, I pull out the small stack of photos I'd been showing to anyone who would look and hold them out.

He doesn't take his eyes off of mine as he steps forward, plucking them from my fingers. I stand rigid and watch as he takes in the image of his daughter for the first time. There's no mistaking she's his. She has his brown eyes, and dark, unruly hair. She even has the little dimple in her chin that I had once teased him about, even though it was one of my favorite features. He swallows thickly and flips to the next photograph, and then the next. All of them are current, and taken within the past few months.

"Her name is Hayden," I say quietly, my heart cracking a little when his eyes fall closed.

"You gave her my last name?"

"And mine," I say, pushing past the pain in his voice as I explain. "Hayden, for your last name, and mine, Dawson. So, Hayden Dawson she is."

I watch as he opens his mouth to speak, but then appears to reconsider, and gives his head a shake. "How long has she been missing?"

"Almost seven hours now," I whisper.

"Jesus." Wyatt glances back down at the photographs. "What can you tell me?"

"She's a computer nut, always has been. She programs video games and other stuff I don't even try to understand. But, a few weeks ago, she started acting really secretive. She'd close her laptop when I came in the room, or she'd be up after her bedtime when she thought I was asleep. None of it was normal for her."

Wyatt pulls a chair away from the desk and brings it closer, indicating for me to take a seat. With a sigh, I move to it and accept the offer, watching as he perches himself on the edge of the bed.

"Then, this afternoon, she didn't return from summer camp. Nobody knew where she was, and the police weren't much help. They figure she's a runaway, but I know my daughter." I ignore the way his jaw hardens at that statement.

"I phoned every friend she has, and all but harassed the police those first few hours, but I got no closer. I got on her laptop, but I can't get on. I'm worried something terrible has happened, Wyatt."

"I'm gonna need that laptop," he says, all business now.

"I have it in my car. I grabbed it before I left to come here."

"Where have you been living?"

I hesitate before answering him. I'd spent so long keeping my whereabouts a secret so he'd never know, and telling him now would go against all that. "Beckettville."

His jaw ticks with anger, but again, he holds back on saying anything. I know he's wondering how we could have been so close all this time and never ran into each other at some point.

"Why didn't the police put out an Amber Alert?"

I sigh. "They wanted to speak with you before they did."

He curses. "I'll speak to them all right. There'll be an Amber Alert out within the hour. Now, go get me that laptop so I can see what she's been up to."

Hashtag

THE SECOND SHELBY is out of my room, the rage inside of me, simmering just below the surface, rips from my chest. With a single swipe of my arm, I shove everything off my work desk, sending it crashing to the floor and against the wall. The thud echoes throughout the room, sounding like a rocket exploding in the night's sky.

"Fuck!" I roar, raking my hand over my face. All these years, she hid my daughter from me, and the only reason her existence was made known to me now is because Shelby needs my help to find her, leaving me only to wonder: what would've happened if she hadn't disappeared? Would she have ever told me?

Now, because of her mother's decision, I may never get the chance to meet her. The one person on this earth with a piece of me inside of her, stolen away before I could even set my eyes on her.

The minutes tick by slowly until Shelby walks back into my room, clutching a hot pink MacBook against her chest like a shield of armor. Her eyes fall to the mess behind me and soften.

"I, uh… here," she stammers, handing it to me. When my fingers graze hers, she recoils from my touch, and fuck if it doesn't hurt, even as pissed as I am. I loved this woman with every fiber of my being. I wanted to make her mine, to give her my last name. Now, as she stands there, she shivers at the idea of breathing the same air as me.

Focus on the girl. Thinking about the past isn't going to fix the present.

"I don't know the password."

"A password has never stopped me before, and it isn't going to now." I retrieve both items from Shelby and set them on my now cleared desk before I turn back to her. "First, we're going to call and get this Amber Alert bullshit taken care of right now."

"You really think you can get them to issue it?"

"You said they needed to talk to her father, which according to you, is me. If that's all that's holding up the process, it should work."

Shelby doesn't move.

"You gonna call them, or are you going to give me this detective's number?" Shelby pulls out her ancient cell phone and presses her finger to the screen. Snatching it from her as the first ring goes through, I put it on speakerphone. "What's this asshole's name?"

"Detective Fischer. Please, don't piss him off. He was less than helpful earlier. I'm worried that if you go all *you* on him, he'll refuse to help at all," she pleads.

"It's his fucking job to help, Shelby. If he'd done his job, there would've been an Amber Alert out hours ago." And then she wouldn't have come to me and turned my life upside down, but I leave that part out.

A voice answers on the second ring. "Beckettville Police Department."

"Yeah, I need to speak to Detective Fischer regarding my missing daughter."

"He's not here right now, sir."

"Then who the fuck's there?" I growl. It's no secret that I hate fucking cops, but this one time, they could prove useful. As I don't have that kind of reach, an Amber Alert will have every single person in the state on the lookout for my girl.

"Please hold. I'll transfer you to one of the detectives on duty."

A few beeps go by before someone else answers. "Detective Moulton."

"Yeah, my kid's missing, and I want to know why the fuck your department is refusing to put an Amber Alert out on her."

"Sir, calm down. Amber Alerts have certain criteria that have to be met before we can issue one. We can't just put one out on any kid who's wandered away from home."

"She hasn't run away," Shelby interjects. "I tried to tell Detective Fischer that, but he wouldn't listen to me."

"What's her name?" he asks.

"Hayden Dawson."

I hear the clicks of the keyboard in the background.

"I'm sorry, but I don't show a report anywhere. Detective Fischer may not have it filed yet in the system, and until he does, there's really nothing I can do. My advice would be to call back in the morning and talk to Fischer directly."

"You've got to be shitting me. All those resources at your fingertips, and you won't do a fucking thing? Your detective told her mother that he'll look into it but needs to talk to me. Well, here the fuck I am. She's not with me. Issue the fucking Amber Alert."

"If you're going to continue to speak to me like that, sir, I'll have to end this call. If you call back and talk to the detective who spoke to your wife, you'll be able to get more answers than I can give you." I ignore his assumption that she's my wife. If she was, this would have never happened. That was Shelby's choice, not mine, and I'm paying the consequences now that she needs my help.

Shelby's eyes plead with me to stop, but I can't. I may not have known about Hayden until tonight, but Shelby's assured me that she's my blood, and a DNA test will prove that later. But even if she isn't, I'm not about to sit around and let the police shove a child's safety on the back burner. I'd been down that road myself, and no child deserves to be ignored by a system meant to protect them from shit like this.

"If you and your department don't want to handle it, I'll fucking do it myself," I bellow before hanging up on the guy. "So help me, Shelby, I'm going to get her back, police or no police. I'll do it." Tears stream down her beautiful face, but I can't focus on her sadness or my rage.

Focus on what you can do. Ignore how much you want to take Shelby into your arms and comfort her.

"Does she have a cell phone?"

"She does, but it wasn't at the house. She never leaves without it."

"What's the number?"

Shelby hesitates. "It's 554-0690."

Opening my desktop, I pull up a geo-locator site I use for the club.

"Service provider?"

"T-Mobile."

My fingers fly across the keyboard, quickly entering in the information and the provider. With a click of the enter key, the screen flashes. My heart drops.

"Her phone hasn't connected to a cell tower since early yesterday morning."

"Oh, God."

"Relax, Shelby. It could mean her phone's off or the battery's dead. We just have to keep checking to see if it connects to a local cell tower, which will get us a close proximity of where she could be or has been. You just have to have a little faith. Let's try her laptop."

My attention goes immediately to the device. I flip it open and the screen lights up. Dozens of strings of green code, like a science fiction movie, cover her home screen, not all that unsimilar to my own setup. "Shit," I mutter, glancing up at Shelby just as the log-in screen pops up with the password box.

"She knows her computers," she confesses with admiration. "Do you think you can get into it?"

"Let me think."

She wasn't kidding. This girl knows her way around a computer and back again. Hayden is definitely not your ordinary twelve-year-old. A strange sense of pride tingles deep in my gut at the realization that I have a daughter who can set up a system like this.

But that means I have to break into it, and there's only two ways I can go about it. The easy way, with Shelby giving me enough information about her for me to crack it, or the hard way, by powering it off and using command prompts to back door my way in, risking the possibility of triggering an internal hard drive wipe, taking everything I'd need with it.

"Tell me something she likes. Television shows, movies, names of her pets, anything you think she would use as a password." My fingers dance over the keyboard, waiting for an answer.

Shelby's lips twist to the side as she thinks. "Oh! We watch *The Bachelor* together."

My head falls. "She's twelve, and she watches that kind of shit? I'm going to pretend I didn't hear that. What else?"

"Marvel movies. She really likes Iron Man."

I try a couple of things: Tony Stark, Iron Man, Jarvis, Happy. I get nothing, except for a warning after the last try. We've only got a couple more tries before it locks me out. Shooting in the dark is now just as risky as trying to back door my way in.

"I'm going to have to try to do this a different way.

It'll take time." Shelby's face falls. "I wish I had a magic wand, but I don't. If I rush this, the hard drive will be wiped, and we'll be up shit's creek."

She tries to hide how anxious she is, but fails. "How long?"

"I should be able to get in there by morning. You can swing back by…" I try to get out before two of the club girls come crashing into my room.

"Hey, Hashy," one of them coos. "You wanna party?" Both of them are drunk as hell, barely able to hold themselves up. Shelby looks between me and the girls with disgust and pain. I start to tell them to leave, but Shelby cuts me off.

"I can't do this. I thought I could for Hayden's sake, but I can't." She bolts for the door, and I try to catch up with her, but the club girls are in the fucking way. I zig and they zag in an attempt to trap me in here with them.

"Move your asses!" I snarl. They jump at the volume of my voice, and scatter from my room like mice running from an exterminator.

By the time I get around them, she's already out the door.

"Haven't seen a piece of ass run away from you that fast in a long time," Karma yells out from across the room. "What did you do? Try that nerdy cosplay out as foreplay?"

"Shut up, asshole. Where's Judge?"

"Something wrong?"

"Yeah, man. My kid's missing."

Karma tilts his head to the side. "You don't have a kid."

"An hour ago, I'd have said the same thing, but shit's changed."

No truer words have I ever spoken. Shit had definitely changed, and I don't know how I feel about that.

Chapter 7

Shelby

THE TEARS ARE DRIED on my cheeks by the time I pull into the house I'd grown up in. *No more,* I scold myself. *You've given that bastard enough of your tears.*

But seeing those girls burst into Wyatt's room was a sharp reminder of why I'd left him in the first place. Of why I couldn't have my daughter anywhere near that kind of lifestyle. The club has been in the news enough as of late, proving that I'd made the right decision for me and my daughter. The reporters never mention them by name, but their calling card is evident. Once you've been on the cusp of their lifestyle, you know exactly who's behind the mayhem.

The look in Wyatt's eyes when I'd told him about Hayden, though… that had just about broken my heart. Such pain, anger, and confusion. Guilt has always niggled away at the back of my mind for keeping Hayden a secret from him, but I'd always managed to find a new excuse for why it had been the right choice. I still think it was the right choice.

But it's not anymore. Something has changed. As much as Wyatt's life—and the women who seem to take up permanent residence in it—hurt me, even I can't deny the intensity he's already shown when it comes to finding our daughter.

Though I'd told my story to several officers, it wasn't until I'd told him about Hayden going missing that I'd finally felt even a modicum of relief. Relief that he was looking. Relief that I wasn't alone. Relief that he had learned about our child and loved her instantly without even meeting her.

When the front door to the house opens, I swipe at my face and fluff my hair before climbing out of the car.

"Hey, Lorna," I say, greeting my stepmother with a false smile and a half-hearted hug.

"Oh, honey," she murmurs, holding me tight to her ample bosom. "I'm so glad you're here."

Another wave of guilt washes over me, but this time, not for the way I'd left Wyatt, but for the way I'd left my dad and Lorna.

I'd spoken to them over the years, of course, but after that horrific night at the clubhouse, I haven't stepped foot back in this town, until now. Dad and Lorna had come to visit every couple of months and stayed for a night or two, but that was the extent of it. And two years ago, when my father had suffered a massive heart-attack on the job and died, even those visits came to an end, and Lorna has been here, alone, ever since.

All I can do is hug her back and force away the fresh wave of tears, praying I don't actually drown in them this time.

"Come in." Taking my hand in hers, she leads me inside.

I'd always liked Lorna. My own mother had deserted me when I was about three years old, leaving me with my dad. He'd raised me and loved me, and did all the things a good parent does. He taught me how to tie my shoes and ride a bike. He taught me how to bait a hook and catch a fish. He'd taught me how to drive.

But luckily for the both of us, Lorna had come along by the time he'd needed to teach me about the growing pains of becoming a woman. And sex. And bras and boys, and thong underwear. Thank God she'd been the one to handle that. I would have been mortified, as well as my dad, if we had to work that out together.

I follow Lorna into the house, and the first thing I notice is that it smells exactly the same. Even the faint smell of Dad's cigars still lingers in the air, likely a permanent smell on every surface in the house.

"Did you see Wyatt?" she asks, leading me to the kitchen and putting the kettle on to boil.

"I did."

For the next hour, I sip on tea and tell her all about how the police had been useless, and about how angry Wyatt had seemed. And I tell her about his promise to find her.

"Do you believe him?"

I stare into her eyes, really considering the question before I answer, "I do." I'm surprised at the truth of that statement. "Wyatt won't stop until he finds her. He may not know her, but I know him. He'll bring her home."

"And then what? What happens then?"

Dropping my face into my hands, I take a deep breath. "I don't know, to be honest. I just don't know."

Lorna gives me a sad smile and places her hand over mine on the table top. "There's still time to think about that, honey. But, in the meantime, let's collect your things and get you upstairs. You look exhausted."

I am exhausted. The last time I'd slept was when Hayden had been asleep, safe in her bed, just down the hall from me. That feels like forever ago. *How am I supposed to sleep not knowing where Hayden is?*

"Go get your stuff and settle in for the night," she

urges. "I got your old room all ready for you." Standing, she carries the cups and teapot to the sink before turning back to me. "You know, the situation may not be the best in these circumstances, but it sure is nice to have you back home, even if it is just for a little while."

This time, I don't have to fake a smile, because as nice as it is for her to have me here, it's unexpectedly nice for me to be back here, in this house. It reminds me of my childhood. Of simpler times. It reminds me of my dad.

"Thank you, Lorna," I say softly before stepping outside to get my overnight bag from the car.

Upstairs, I push open the door to my old bedroom, and for a moment, I can't breathe.

Everything is the same. Like, literally everything. My Justin Timberlake poster is still hanging proudly next to Beyoncé. The pom poms I'd kept from my senior year pep rally still sit on my bookshelf. Even my old CD player sits proudly on top of my dresser. It's like going back in time.

My single bed is made perfectly, with my ruffled bedspread laid out on top of it. It looks heavenly.

I don't waste another moment getting ready. In record time, I climb into my nightgown, brush my teeth, and use the facilities. And then, in a moment of pure nostalgia, I peel back the blankets on my childhood bed and climb into it.

When my head hits the pillow, I remember the determination on Wyatt's face as he plucked away at the keys on Hayden's computer. That memory is the one thing that gives me the permission I need to finally fall into a deep, much-needed sleep.

Hashtag

"I NEED to take some time off," I state, just as the last of my brothers take their seats around our meeting room table. Judge's stare hardens, and he crosses his arms across his chest.

"And what's that supposed to mean?"

"Exactly what I just said. Something's come up, and I need to focus on it." It's not every day that a patch asks for time off. When you take your patch, you're dedicating yourself to the brotherhood. You can't just walk away from it like it's some normal nine-to-five job, but I have no choice. Hayden needs my undivided attention.

Judge's eyes narrow. "Don't think I didn't see who crashed the party tonight, Hash. What kind of trouble is she in?"

"It's not Shelby, Prez."

"Then what the fuck is this all about? This isn't a job. You don't have vacation time." His voice comes out as a commanding growl. Part of me thought I could just walk in here and request a couple of weeks off with zero questions. Clearly, that part of me is a fucking idiot with his head stuck in the Shelby Dawson fucks-up-my-life cloud again.

"Tell 'em, Hash," Karma interjects, prodding me to spill it. The last thing I want to do is drag my club into my personal shit, but I don't really have a choice.

"Fine," I growl. "I want to make it clear right now that this isn't the club's problem. I have a kid, and she's missing."

"Shit, man," GP mutters.

"That's why Shelby came to me. She needs my help to find her, and thinks she's been kidnapped by someone she's been talking to online."

"Why didn't she go to the police?"

"She did, but they were no help. She hasn't been missing long enough for them to take action. They won't even issue an Amber Alert."

"Sounds like the bitch's problem if you ask me," Stone Face huffs.

"I must've misheard you, because I know you didn't just call her a bitch." The fire inside of me roars to life, and it takes every single ounce of control I have not to fly over the table and lay the big motherfucker out.

"Dude, I'd shut up if I were you," GP snaps. "You don't want to stir that shit pot." Damn right he doesn't. He doesn't know the first thing about Shelby and I's history. Not many of my club does outside of Judge, GP, and Karma.

"I didn't stutter."

Before I can put the brakes on, I'm out of my chair, chest heaving, but Stone Face doesn't move from his fucking chair. I don't know what his damn problem is, but I'm about to fix it with my fist going down his throat. "Call her a bitch one more time, I'll beat that word right out of your limited vocabulary."

GP pinches the bridge of his nose. "Here we go."

Karma reaches into his pocket and whips out his wallet, fingers a twenty-dollar bill, and tosses it onto the table in front of him. "I got twenty on Stone whipping his ass."

"Enough!" Judge yells, shoving himself out of his chair at the head of the table. "Both of you. Sit down and shut the fuck up!"

I glare over at Stone Face as I sit down. This isn't the end of this conversation. For a man of so few words, he sure has a lot to say about my ex, a woman he doesn't know at all. *Do I really even know her?* Shelby isn't mine. She doesn't wear my patch. Am I really willing to put my own patch on the line to defend her?

"Now that you two have finished your pissing match, your request is denied, Hash."

I start to argue, but Judge glares at me, lifting his palm in the air. "Do you know who has her? Any reason to believe it's a club motivated kidnapping?"

Shit. I hadn't even thought of that. "Doubtful they would know about her if I didn't, but I can't rule it out, Prez. Not until I access the laptop Shelby gave me."

Judge nods. "See what you can find and report back. You may not want to involve the club, but I'm not giving you a choice. She's your blood, and that makes her a part of our family." He glances over at Stone Face. "We protect our own. If she's really in trouble, we've got his back."

"I appreciate that, Prez."

"Anything else we need to discuss?" The room remains silent, and with a hit of his gavel against the table, we're dismissed. A few of the guys offer their support as we file out of the room, while the rest of them return to the party. I head straight back to my room.

Stepping inside, I close the door behind me, eyeing Hayden's pink laptop. *Time to get to work and find my daughter.* As I walk toward my work desk, I yell out a command to my voice-controlled sound system, and within a few seconds, Black Stone Cherry begins to pour out of my speakers.

Settling in for what could be a long night, I wait for the screen to load, type in the first command prompt, and hit the enter key. It buzzes at me. *Denied.*

"Okay," I mutter under my breath. "Let's try this one." I type it in, and the second I hit enter, it buzzes again. *Denied.* "Third time's the charm?" The third one goes in, and the wheel spins for a split second, giving me hope, until the same buzz greets me.

Fuck, she's better than I was at her age, and that's saying something. I was backdooring my way into my school's aging servers to change my grades at her age. If she can do this, what else is she capable of? Pride would be swelling inside my gut again if I didn't need to get into her laptop so badly.

I crack my knuckles before I key in a different prompt, one I haven't used in years. "Come on, let me in," I mutter, hitting the enter key one more time. This time, the home screen pops up.

"I'm in!"

Wasting no time, I start looking through her browsing history. Her Google searches are atypical of what I'd normally think a twelve-year-old would be interested in. Alienware computers and coding online courses litter her history. I'd half expected to see YouTube videos, and even that fucking TikTok app I keep seeing everywhere. Nothing is out of the ordinary. Well, except the one search for *The Bachelor* spoilers, but I ignore that. A few scrolls more and I hit pay dirt. A message board for an online video game starts showing up repeatedly. Clicking on the most recent link, I find a conversation about cheat codes for a game called Blox World.

I switch over to her desktop and find a link to the application there. Clicking it, the game begins to load, and while it does, I open up my cell phone and pull up the information about it. Blox World, it turns out, is an interactive game for kids with interests in game development and coding. They can create their own worlds, and allow other users to test out their creations. Its setup allows even the most uneducated kid the opportunity to dip their toes into creating a world of their own. I'd have loved this kind of thing growing up.

Peering back up at the computer screen, I see the game has finally loaded, thankfully logging directly into her own game without the need of another password. A few chat windows pop open.

BearClaw220: Nice world building.

DrewD21: Can you meet me tomorrow before summer camp? I need help with programming my rocket launch sequence. Please, H?

It's the last one that piques my interest, dated for this

morning, hours before she disappeared, per Shelby.

P4r4D0X: Can't wait for later!

Bingo. I pull up her account history and see that she's talked to this particular user a lot. More than a lot—every single day. I try to open some of the past conversations, but an error pops up when I click on them. I click on his username, but the information is blank, which isn't surprising, since nowadays, game developers have built safeguards for kids from sharing their personal information, which begs the question: how did they go from online to offline?

Mulling it over, I lean back in my chair. If there are safeguards, like I assume, she had to have figured out a way to get around them. I pull up the chat with Bear-Claw220 to test my theory. I type in a fake phone number, and as soon as I hit enter, the number is replaced with stars in the chat box. I try a fake address this time, and the same thing happens. How did they go from online to offline if Shelby's suspicions are right? Furthermore, why wasn't she monitoring her computer time? No child at Hayden's age should have free access to a computer without some kind of parental lock or supervision. The online world is dangerous for kids. If Shelby is right about where Hayden may be, there's only one question I have.

Why didn't she protect our daughter?

Chapter 9

Shelby

I'M sound asleep when the door to my bedroom crashes open, causing my heart to nearly leap out of my chest. "What the hell?" I cry, sitting up in bed, suddenly wide awake.

Lorna stands in the hallway, barely visible over a hulking Wyatt, who's already moving toward my bed. "I'm sorry," she says. "I tried to stop him."

"I'm done being stopped by you fucking people," Wyatt snaps at her, flinging the door closed.

I scowl as I swing my legs over the side of the bed. "You didn't have to be so rude."

Wyatt snorts and folds his arms over his broad chest. "Like hell. That old witch is part of the reason I don't know about my own damn kid. Besides, you have to show respect to get it, and she's never shown me any of that."

I suddenly become aware of the situation I'm in at this moment. A tiny room, a single bed, wearing nothing but a white tank top and pink panties. "Can you wait in the hallway?" I rasp, pulling the blanket up to cover myself.

He smirks. "What's wrong, Shel? Don't want me to see you without a bra? I mean, it's not like I haven't seen them before."

"Just go wait in the hall," I hiss, tossing a pillow at his head.

Snatching it out of the air, he chuckles as he disappears through the door, closing it behind him. *Asshole.*

As soon as I hear the latch click, I hop off the bed and rush to my overnight bag. I dig through it, pulling out an off-white bra and a worn pair of jeans. I use the en suite bathroom and quickly brush my teeth and wash my face.

My purple-hued hair is short, and takes only a little effort to have it laying just right. Deciding to forgo the make-up, I slip my hand through a dozen or so silver bangles and open the bedroom door.

Wyatt's gaze starts down at my toes and slowly glides back up to my face. "You don't look much different, other than all the tattoos."

I love tattoos. There's something about commemorating important events in your life, or showing the world your soul through permanent art on your skin. It's always fascinated me.

"I own a shop," I inform him. "That way, when I run out of places on my own skin, I can ink up other people." I look him up and down. "I see you still don't have any."

"This body is a fucking temple. No way in hell is anything important enough to make me desecrate it."

I scan the body he so casually referred to, and he's right. It is a temple. It's chiseled, hard, and broad, and easily the sexiest male body I've ever seen. I'd love the opportunity to mark it with my tattoo gun—*amongst other things.*

"See something you like?"

Shit. "What exactly are you doing here at…"—I check my phone. Wow, I'd definitely been tired—"… eleven o'clock in the morning?"

Wyatt takes in my bedroom in all its early millennium charm, and frowns. "Can we talk somewhere else? Pretty sure the boy band posters are eye fucking me."

A snort of laughter escapes through my nose in the most unladylike fashion, making Wyatt grin. "Downstairs," I say through my chuckle. "We can sit out on the patio."

As we hit the main floor, I see Lorna peering around the corner with worry creasing her wrinkled forehead. I give her a tight smile and point to the rear of the house to indicate our plans. I catch her nod just before I step outside into the late morning sun.

The metal chairs are starting to rust around the edges, but Lorna has kept the cushions in perfect condition over the years. I plop down in one of the chairs and wait for Wyatt to sit across from me.

"What did you find?"

Wyatt sighs. "Not a lot, to be honest. Still no signal on her phone. I did manage to get into her computer, though." He leans forward. "Did she ever mention a game she liked to play called Blox World?"

I sit back and think. "Yes, she loved that game. She talked about it all the time, but she spoke about a lot of things she did online. I didn't understand any of it."

"Kids build worlds," he persists, "talk to each other. Hang out. It's a coder kid's wet dream."

My nose wrinkles. "Ew, gross. And besides, Hayden's a girl. She has boobs, not wet dreams."

Wyatt's eyes narrow at the idea of his daughter having breasts. "Anyway," he scowls, clearly not wanting to stay on that topic any longer. "It seems Hayden's been playing it quite a bit, and talking to one user daily for a while. The last message said, from whomever it was, that they couldn't wait for later. It was sent yesterday morning."

Tears prick at my eyes. All along, I'd been telling

everyone that someone had taken her, but Wyatt's words have just confirmed it.

"Shelby, she was on that game at all hours of the day and night. Do you not monitor her online time?"

I gape at him. "Are you saying this is my fault?"

"No, I'm asking a fucking question."

I press my hands to the arms of the chair, both to steady myself—as my world spins out of control—and to keep myself from lunging at this man for even insinuating I don't take proper care of my daughter.

"Shelby is a straight A student. She does her chores, follows the rules, and never talks back. I trust her. Why would I monitor her online time? I don't know a damn thing about the internet."

His face softens. "And that's exactly why she needs to be monitored. Online is the easiest place for a girl like her to fall victim to a predator."

A sob wracks my entire body, and the tears I'd been fighting spill over. "What are we going to do?"

"We need a lawyer. We need the chat threads for Hayden's account, all of them. We need to get a court order to get them from the game developer of Blox World."

Hashtag

"THIS IS THE PLACE." Shelby pulls her car up to the curb of a large brick building near downtown. A large gold and black sign sits just outside of it with large letters reading *Stratford and Goldman* in block print. The sign alone screams expensive. It seems she's got friends in high places.

"How did you get an appointment so fast?" I question. Unless she has an attorney on retainer, she shouldn't have been able to book a same day appointment. The longer I think about it, the more I feel on edge. Shelby opens the door and slides out from behind the wheel without answering me.

"What the fuck?" I growl, reaching for the handle and bolting out of the passenger side, racing to catch up to her. Her heels click against the pavement as we approach the front of the building.

"Shelby!" I call out to her. Stopping, she spins around to face me. "I asked you a question back there, and you bolt out of the car like your hair's on fire. What's going on?"

"The sooner we get in there, the closer we'll be to getting Hayden back." She chews on her bottom lip, just like she used to when she was nervous. We both want Hayden back—me more than anything—but there's something else, lingering below the surface that she isn't saying, and it's bothering me. What am I about to walk in to?

"There's something you're not telling me."

"It's not important."

"If you're gnawing on your lip, it's important." Shelby releases her lip, and it's red. Redder than I've ever seen it before.

"Come on, we're going to be late." Dismissing my hesitation, she charges forward and through the darkened glass doors. With a shake of my head, I tag along behind her until she stops at the reception desk in the center of the room.

"Name, please?" the perky little brunette behind the desk asks, her eyes growing wide when she notices me standing behind Shelby. I've seen that look a dozen times before. She's hungry for something a little more danger-ous, something off her normal menu. Shelby's body tenses ever so slightly, and had I not been paying more attention to her than the little brunette, I would have missed it. Too bad for her, she isn't on my radar, but she's now on Shelby's.

"Dawson. I'm here to see K—I mean, Mrs. Stratford. We have an appointment."

"One moment, please." Her fingers click over the keyboard, but her eyes linger on me for a few seconds longer before she peers at her screen. "Ah, yes. Her assistant called earlier with instructions for you to meet Mrs. Stratford in her private conference room. She should be joining you momentarily. Just take the elevator to the top floor." She points a finger to the elevators, left of the reception hall. "Or, if you'd like a personal escort, I'd be happy to take you up."

"No," Shelby nearly growls, but quickly covers it up. "We can manage it on our own." She turns to look at me over her shoulder before heading toward the aforemen-tioned elevators. Her red, manicured finger presses against the button to call it at least a half a dozen times. I stifle a chuckle under my breath, but she catches me and scowls.

The elevator dings when it arrives. Once the doors slide open, we both step inside, silence encasing the small space between us as she bounces nervously on her heels.

"Still don't like elevators?" I take a step closer to her, decreasing the space between us. "What if I do this?" I hop into the air, and she squeals when I land.

"You know how much I hate that, Wyatt."

"Just trying to lighten the mood, sweetheart." I shrug. "After that display of yours in the lobby, I thought you could use a laugh."

"I don't know what you're talking about." *Oh, yes you do.* She can try to hide it all she wants, but there's still something there, even if she doesn't want to admit it. "I just didn't want to be late to our meeting."

"You're cute when you try to lie." Her nostrils flare just enough to confirm it. She's pissed that the receptionist took notice of me, and outwardly flirted right in front of her.

The elevator dings, and the doors slide open. Taking the opportunity to end the conversation, she exits. I step out of the elevator and onto what I can only assume is the executive level of the firm. A thin woman is greeting Shelby near the entrance of a large room when I approach, her face lighting up with fear when she sees me. Apparently, it's not every day a biker walks into the penthouse suite of a firm like this.

Shelby turns to me with a serious look on her beautiful face. "Promise me, you won't ruin this."

I arch my brow, the uneasiness I felt earlier returning as I process her request. "Ruin what? All this lawyer friend of yours needs to do is their job, and everything will be fine."

"Please, Wyatt." Her voice wavers ever so slightly.

"What aren't you telling me?"

Just over Shelby's shoulder, the door to the conference room opens, and on the other side is someone I never wanted to see again—Kasey.

"No fucking way. We're leaving." I reach for Shelby's arm, but she jerks away from me, digging in her heels on her decision to consult with the bane of my existence about my daughter.

Kasey smiles. "I see nothing has changed with you, Wyatt. All these years, and you're still playing a biker in your little biker gang. How are you not in prison?"

She eyes me up and down, just like she used to do when we were in high school. No matter how successful I could have been, I would never have measured up in Kasey's eyes. Not that I've ever cared one fucking wink about what she thinks of me.

"Let's move this conversation into the conference room. I don't want to disturb my high-profile clients with this kind of unpleasantness." Kasey moves farther into the room, leaving Shelby and I alone.

"Wyatt," Shelby begs, a tear rolling down her face. "Please. We need her help."

"Shelby, she's the last person on earth I would ever ask a favor of, even for Hayden." If Kasey is my only law-abiding option, I'll find another way, with or without a court order.

"We need to try, Wyatt. You said it yourself that developers like this one don't open their user list to anyone. We need that court order to get the records, and Kasey can do that for us."

"Then why did you come to me if Kasey can help you? Why did you drag me into this?"

"Because you're Hayden's father, and the only person who could have gotten us to this point. Kasey can help us move that needle ahead. Please, you just have to talk to her and see what she can do."

"I don't like this. I don't like that you lied to my face about just who this attorney friend of yours is, and I don't like that you hid my daughter from me until you needed my help. In fact, I fucking hate all of this."

"I know, but if we want to get this information, Kasey is the only attorney who can do it without waiting weeks for an appointment. She's our only option."

The only *legal* option she means. Before I even went

to see her this morning, I'd considered sending a couple of the guys over to the developer's office for a "friendly" meeting, but it was a risk. They could give us nothing in return. But with a court order, they'd have to hand over the information.

"Fine," I growl. "But I need you to understand that if she opens that mouth of hers and spits out shit at me like she just did, I will walk and do this my way."

With my reluctant agreement, I step inside the room with Shelby following behind me, closing the door. Kasey sits at the head of a large table with chairs tucked underneath each side. Just breathing the same air as this woman sends a course of rage sliding up my spine.

"Take a seat." Kasey outstretches her hand to the empty seats next to her. Shelby settles into one, but I park my ass several more down, away from her. Taking notice of my placement, she rolls her eyes. "You don't have to sit so far away, Wyatt." Her voice is slick with contentment. She knows she got to me out there with her comment, playing right into her intent to piss me off.

"I'm close enough."

Kasey turns her attention to Shelby and grips her hand tightly, her eyes softening as she looks at her. "Everything okay? You sounded upset when you called earlier, but I didn't expect to hear you say you needed to see me, and that you'd be bringing him along."

"It's Hayden, Kase."

Kasey's eyes grow wide at the mention of my daughter's name. "Does he…?"

"Yes, he knows. She was taken, Kase. Wyatt thinks she was chatting with someone on this game she likes to play, but we need a court order to get access to the user's information to track him down."

"Why didn't you come to me first? You didn't need to involve him with this, not after all these years."

That's when it hits me that Kasey knows about Hayden. How is that possible, unless… No. Shelby wouldn't have done that to me.

"How does she know about Hayden, Shelby?" I say quietly, slowly pushing away from the table. Guilt is clear on her face. "Tell me. You owe me that much."

"Wyatt, please. Now isn't the time."

"When would've been a good time to know that I had a kid? You've had twelve years to tell me, yet she knew before I did. I'm her fucking father, Shelby!"

"And where were you when she was born, Wyatt? Riding with your biker gang? What kind of life is that to raise a baby in? I gave Shelby and Hayden what you couldn't—safety."

Pointing in Kasey's direction, I growl, "She was fucking there when Hayden was born and not me?"

"Wyatt…" She trails off, lowering her head.

"Who do you think rescued her from you?" Kasey spits out. "Someone had to be there for her."

As soon as the words leave her mouth, the thin grip I had on my self-control slips and cracks. I could have forgiven Shelby for a lot of things, but not this. There's no coming back from this lie.

"It's one thing that you hid my daughter from me until she vanished under your lack of parental control, but this? Her? I can't." I pivot on my heels and start for the door, stopping just short of ripping it off its hinges.

"Where are you going?" Shelby cries out.

"To find my daughter."

I walk out the door without bothering to look back. There's nothing left for me in that room now.

Shelby

"I SEE he hasn't changed much," Kasey huffs, plopping down into the nearest seat, crossing her feet atop the mahogany conference table. "Honestly, though," she continues. "Why would you go to him instead of me?"

I can't take it anymore. "Damnit, Kasey! Did you not hear what I said?" Reaching out, I shove her feet off the table, feeling only slightly better when they hit the floor with a thunk that makes Kasey wince. "Hayden is missing. Gone. Kidnapped. Very likely being trafficked as we speak. Why the hell does it matter who I went to? Just do what you can to help me find my baby girl, okay?"

Kasey's brown eyes are grave as she leans forward and takes my hand. "I'm sorry, Shel. Of course, you're right. You mentioned a game. What game, and what do you need?"

Relief washes over me as she pulls out a pad of paper and a pen. The feud between Wyatt and Kasey had always been hard on me, and for them to continue that now while my daughter's in danger isn't going to fly. Everyone has a reason to be angry in this scenario, but this is simply not the time to let that play out.

I take a seat beside her, and for the next few minutes, I tell her everything that Wyatt had found. I tell her about Blox World, and give her Hayden's username. It takes her all of three minutes to do an internet search on the game developers to link it to a company she can subpoena for the activity records.

"You leave this with me, Shel. I know a judge who will take care of this for me right away. He owes me a favor."

"I'm so fucking scared, Kasey." A fat, hot tear escapes the corner of my eye and slides slowly down my cheek. "What if she's hurt? Or what if we don't find her? What if—"

"Shh, we'll find her," she assures me. "Hayden's a smart kid. And as much as I hate to admit it, Wyatt's a smart guy. He won't let that happen. Whoever has her doesn't know what they're in for."

Sniffing, I manage a small smile and push out of my chair. "I'd better go. We need that information, Kasey, and we need it fast."

Wrapping her arms around my shoulders, she holds me tight. "I'm on it, Shel. You know I love that not-so-little girl. We'll get her back."

"Thank you," I whisper, giving a small wave as I slip out the door and down the long, formal corridor.

Knowing that Kasey is on the job brings me a small sense of relief, but that feeling is far outweighed by the anger I feel at Wyatt right now. And the worst part is, I don't know if I even have the right to be angry with him.

He, however, has a right to be angry with me, seeing as how I kept his daughter a secret from him all this time. But he promised me we would deal with that later. He promised that finding Hayden would be our main priority.

So why did he have such a fit over Kasey? Why would he let his anger and pride get in the way of help to bring Hayden home? To me, that had been a truly selfish act, proving I'd been right about his ability to parent all along. A parent can't let pride dictate how they raise their child. A parent needs to swallow down those feelings and do whatever it takes to be the best they can be for their kids.

I push my way out the front door of the office, and there, leaning against my car, is the object of my anger. Wyatt's arms are folded across his chest as he scowls at me.

"I thought you left," I bite out through clenched teeth.

"Well, I can't exactly walk home from here now, can I?"

I unlock just the driver's side door and open it. "I don't give a fuck what you do, Wyatt. You can fly home with a broomstick up your ass for all I care."

He opens his mouth to speak, but I don't give him a chance to finish. Dropping down into the driver's seat, I slam the door, closing me off to whatever he was saying. His hand is on the passenger's side door handle, giving it a tug, but it's still locked.

"Shelby, open the damn door." He knocks on the window, meeting my eyes through the glass. "I get it, you're pissed, but I'm pissed too. I'm pissed about so many things right now, and I don't have a fucking clue how to ignore it until we find Hayden. But I'm trying, okay? Which is more than you've ever allowed me to do before."

Starting the engine, I grip the steering wheel as he talks. And then, my own thought from a few minutes ago comes floating back through my mind like a taunt. *A parent needs to swallow down those feelings and do whatever it takes to be the best they can be for their kids.*

"Fuck," I growl as I jab my finger down on the button to unlock the door.

Once inside, he mutters, "Thank you," not sounding very thankful at all.

"Sitting here arguing with each other isn't getting Hayden home any quicker."

Wyatt stews in his own frustrations most of the way home, but even I can't be so lucky as for him to stay quiet the entire way.

"How could you keep this from me, Shelby?" His voice is filled with both raw pain and anger. "You knew I wanted a family. You knew I wanted to have kids some-day. You knew I wanted to do all of that with you."

I turn onto Lorna's street, trying to restrain myself from going any faster. "Wyatt, don't."

"Don't what? Don't ask questions? Don't wonder? Don't expect a fucking answer?"

My jaw's clenched so tight, pain radiates throughout it, and my blood feels like it may boil over at any moment. "Don't ask questions you don't want truthful answers to."

Throwing his head back, he belts out the most humor-less laugh I've ever heard, but I ignore him as I pull up in front of Lorna's house. I need to get away from him. I need to put an end to this discussion.

As soon as the car comes to a stop, I throw it in park and get out, speed walking toward the front door before Wyatt can even put one foot on the ground. "You wouldn't know truth if it jumped up and bit you on the ass!" he hollers at my back.

Those words stop me in my tracks. This man is preaching to me about truth? The same man who knocked me up and had a threesome with a pair of skanks? *Fuck that.*

Turning slowly, I make sure his gaze is locked with mine before I speak. I speak slowly and clearly, my words like a sharp sword, aimed and ready for battle. "You want to know the real truth, Wyatt? You want to know why I didn't tell you about Hayden?"

He stands frozen in place, his eyes never leaving mine. I think back to the day I'd tried to call him. Hayden was only three days old, and I hadn't slept for any of it. My conscience had gotten the better of me, and I had picked up the phone.

But it wasn't Wyatt who answered—it was Layla. We all grew up together, and I knew her voice. I never left a message. Hell, I never said a word. I just hung up, unable to believe what had happened to the life I'd so desperately wanted.

"You made your choice before I ever left. You chose that club, that family. You chose to live a life I never wanted."

"You supported me while I was prospecting. What the hell changed?"

"You," I snap back. "You changed. You changed into the kind of man who should never have a child. The kind of man who would make a terrible father, and an even worse partner. You're the last man on earth I'd want helping me raise my child. Hayden deserves better than someone like you as a father."

My words hit their mark. I know it the instant his shoulders drop that I'd struck a mortal blow. He stares at me with so much hurt and confusion, I almost want to take my words and stuff them back into my mouth. But once something like that is spoken, it can never be unheard.

"I'll let you know what I find out," he says, his eyes dropping to the ground in front of me. "You let me know if you hear anything."

With my lips pressed together, I can only manage a nod as he turns and swings his leg over his motorcycle. It's not until he rides out of sight that I realize I may have won that argument, but it was at Wyatt's expense. I broke something there. I should've kept my big mouth shut.

Chapter 12

Hashtag

THE LAST MAN *on earth that she'd want helping her raise her child. Someone like you.*

Shelby's harsh words rattle inside my head as I ride back to the clubhouse.

I'm not perfect, and she knew that all those years ago. I didn't give a shit about what people thought of me. I had enough of those lectures from my foster parents to last me a lifetime. They saw a troubled boy itching for trouble, not the intelligent child who was begging to be given the same opportunities as every other kid. Too smart for my own good, yet too poor to be successful.

But Judge didn't see me that way. He saw my potential, and gave me the tools I needed to succeed. No matter how many people tried to tell me I was a fucking idiot for prospecting for the Black Hoods, it was, and still is, the right decision for me. This club, and the men in it, changed my life.

They're my home.

My family.

The one thing I wanted most in the world—to belong to something bigger. To just *belong*.

Yet in a single sentence, Shelby had me reeling in anger, second-guessing every single fucking decision I've ever made. Would she have stuck around and allowed me to be in my daughter's life if I was more like everyone else? A normal man with a normal life? A mind-numbing, meaningless existence with a big house, white picket fence, and an HOA?

Fuck normal. Fuck her.

I am who I am, and if that makes me a shitty candidate for fatherhood, she probably should have thought about that before dating a guy like me, let alone fucking me for three solid years up to that point. She knew the risk, we both did, but that sure as hell didn't stop her from hopping into bed with me.

I pull into the clubhouse and park my Harley near the rear entrance. The place is as silent as the grave, which is normal for this time of day. Most of the guys have side gigs they work on when the club hits a slow period. The only bike that sits in the parking lot is Judge's. With another look around to see if the coast is clear, I head over to the makeshift shooting range near the edge of the property.

Near a patio table at the edge of the range sits several boxes of empty beer bottles. I finger a few of them and walk down to the fence row, placing five on the top before walking back to the table. Retrieving my gun from the back of my jeans, I fire a shot. It ricochets off the rocky wall behind the fence post.

"Fuck!" I exclaim, firing another. It misses again. I rapid fire three more shots, but only one hits its mark.

A crunch of gravel sounds from behind me as I pull my extra magazine from my holder and load it in. I rack the slide back when Judge appears next to me.

"Nice shooting," he mutters sarcastically. "Your aim still needs work."

I ignore him, firing off a couple more rounds, and finally take out one of the beer bottles, shattering it to bits.

"Something on your mind, Hash?" Pulling out his own gun, he fires off four quick shots, breaking the remaining bottles.

"Why would there be?" I go back to the empty beer case and retrieve another five bottles. I take my time putting them where they need to go, repeating what I did with the first set. Finally, I return back to the head of the range where Judge still stands.

"Most of the guys come out here to practice," he adds, firing another couple of shots. "You, on the other hand, only come out here when you need to blow off steam."

He's not wrong. I may not be a dead shot like the other guys, but there's something therapeutic about it, like controlled destruction in an already chaotic world. It clears my mind and lets me focus on the problem in front of me. I wish that was the case for Hayden and Shelby. There aren't enough bottles in the world to help me calm the raging storm inside of me when it comes to Shelby.

His boots crunch into the gravel. *Shit.* He's not leaving.

"Hit a couple of brick walls with tracking down my daughter," I grumble, firing several shots back to back, my rage spilling over the edge with each one. "It's being worked out."

"You were always a shit liar, Wyatt. The longer you keep sitting on that powder keg inside your head, the worse it'll be when you explode. Get it out, son."

"Hayden had been playing an online game. I found a message that leads me to believe she was meeting up with another player that day. The user was wiped from her system."

"What's the problem, then? Do that computer wizardry shit you do and get the guy's information."

"It's not that simple. Games like this are huge, with millions of players in one online space. The only way I can get that information is by subpoenaing the developer who hosts it."

"Go talk to another attorney. Club's been needing to hire a new one since Gary quit practicing a few years back. We'll pay for it."

"We went to see one this morning who's an old friend of Shelby's. One who used to frequent the club back in my prospecting days."

"The mouthy brunette?" he inquires. "Skinny little thing with no tits?"

"That's the one. I walked right into her office without a fucking clue as to who we were meeting."

"That girl was always a thorn in my side whenever she came to the clubhouse. She stirred up the hang-arounds and the guys," Judge chuckles. "Hell, you damn near lost the patch vote because of her. A couple of the guys were on the fence, wondering if she'd be sticking around if we patched you."

"Trust me, if she and Shelby weren't a package deal back then, I'd have helped you throw her ass out." Right into a barrel of starving piranhas. Though knowing she was a part of Shelby's escape plan, piranhas would be too merciful.

"Did she refuse to help you?"

"She was a cold-hearted bitch about it, but she's going to help," I answer flatly.

"Then I guess I have to ask: what's the problem? Seems like tracking down your daughter is progressing."

"It's Shelby. One second, we're a united front. Next thing I know, I'm public enemy number one."

"Fuck Shelby."

I arch an eyebrow at him.

"That shit between you and her doesn't matter, dumbass. You need to focus on finding your kid."

"That's what I'm trying to do," I huff, tossing my arms up in the air. "But one conversation with her is like having knives driven under my fingernails. I can't move past it."

Judge shakes his head and looks to the ground. "Take it from an old man. Women and bitches come and go, but blood means everything. That connection means fucking everything. Not one person in the world can take that away from your kid, not even her mother."

"You speaking from experience, Prez?"

"I had a son once. Best damn thing that could've ever happened to me. The second he took his first breath, it was like everything inside of me lived for him."

"What happened?"

"He died forty-three days after he was born from SIDS." Judge aims his gun and blows three more bottles to bits. When he's done, he continues. "Happened when I was out on a ride with the club in my prospecting days. My ex buried him before I got back. To this day, I don't even know where his grave is. Won't ever know. She took his location with her to her grave a few years back."

"Shit, man. I had no idea."

"No one does, and it better stay that way."

"Sure, Judge."

Clapping his large hand on my shoulder, he squeezes it hard. "Your daughter needs you to find her, and you're the best shot she has. All this shit with her mom, forget about it. Shove it aside. Use that anger inside of you to focus on what you need to do. That's how you find her."

Without another word, he releases me and walks away from the range, leaving me alone. I aim my gun, but it falls against my side.

The system failed me the second they put me into foster care after my druggie of a mom overdosed in a Wendy's parking lot, with me in the back seat. I can't change that, but I *can* change Hayden's fate.

I can't fail her. Not now, not ever. Failure isn't an option.

Chapter 13

Shelby

"WELL, AS I LIVE AND BREATHE," Lorna cries from the front porch. "Would you look at you, girl! Come and give me a hug."

The sounds of Lorna greeting Kasey float throughout the house, and I stand from my place at the kitchen table, where I'd been unsuccessfully making phone call after phone call to more kids from Hayden's class, hoping they'd heard from her.

"She's right in here." Lorna's high-pitched voice alerts me that they're on their way.

Lorna enters the kitchen first, and Kasey shoots me an apologetic smile as she comes in behind her.

"Sorry to burst in on you ladies." Kasey wraps her arms around my shoulders and pulls me into a hug. I don't hug her back. It's been less than twelve hours since

I'd seen her last, which means she likely has news. With so little time having passed, I'm not betting that it's good news.

"I heard back from Judge Onstein just a little while ago," she says, taking my hands in hers. "It took a little convincing, but he was sympathetic to the situation. He made the phone calls himself, and Blox World has already been served papers, and has been instructed to send over the information you were looking for as soon as possible."

I can only gape at her. "Isn't that too easy?"

She grins. "Not when your husband's uncle is a Supreme Court Judge. I just hope they don't take their sweet time getting those files into our hands, and that once we have them, there's something there that will help us find Hayden."

My face crumples as my daughter's name leaves her lips. "Oh, Kasey," I cry. "What if we can't find her?"

Lorna pulls me into a hug as Kasey crosses her arms over her chest, glaring down her nose at me. "Uh-uh, not happening. Not yesterday, and not today. There won't be any pity party on my watch. You want to crumble? You do it after Hayden's safe in her bed. All that fear you have going on in there right now, save it. It's not the time."

Lorna holds me tighter, attempting to shield me from Kasey's words. "Her daughter is missing," she admonishes, lowering her voice on the last word as if it's too filthy to say aloud.

"Yes, she is," Kasey agrees, placing one hand on my back, and the other on Lorna's. "And she needs her momma to keep it together."

I sniff, knowing full well she's right. "I'm so tired of crying all the damn time," I tell them both.

"Then don't." Kasey has no clue what it's like to have a daughter missing. Hell, she doesn't even have kids.

"Honey," Lorna interrupts. "You wanna cry, you cry. You wanna yell, you yell. You want to punch somebody …" She trails off. "Punch Miss Kasey here."

"Hey!" Kasey cries, a smile spreading across her face. I can't help but chuckle.

"I like that idea."

She laughs. "Figures you would."

Lorna gives me a squeeze and pulls away, wiping at a few stray tears. "I think this calls for a stiff drink. What do you girls think?"

Kasey and I lock eyes over Lorna's head, our eyebrows raised high. As one, we burst into full-blown, belly shaking laughter. Lorna jumps a little at the sudden noise, looking first at Kasey, and then at me, confusion twisting her withered face. And then she joins us, her joyous cackle making us laugh even harder.

I laugh so hard, my lungs hurt. But the lack of oxygen

doesn't even matter. The past couple of days have been the hardest days of my life. Fear had overwhelmed me, nearly breaking my spirit. But when strait-laced Lorna suggested a stiff drink, the laughter that followed was a blessed relief.

"You girls are just as crazy as you were when you were sixteen years old," she declares, stalking to the cupboard and pulling out three crystal tumblers. "Pick your poison. I've got whiskey, vodka, and some vanilla bean moonshine."

Kasey widens her eyes at me before holding up a hand and calling out, "Moonshine!"

"Moonshine for me too," I giggle.

We watch in shock as Lorna pulls out a step stool. Climbing to the top, she reaches deep into the cupboard and pulls out a large jug of yellow liquid. Like a professional bartender, she uses tiny silver tongs to place ice cubes into the tumblers and pours the liquid over top.

She hands us our glasses and holds hers up in the air, and I can't help but notice it holds more moonshine than ours. "Bottoms up."

"Bottoms up," we repeat, but Lorna's already well into chugging hers. So much for moonshine being something you sip. Apparently, Lorna's become a boozer since my father passed away.

"So, Kasey," she says, her cheeks already starting to

flush from the alcohol. "Have you had a chance to see Wyatt since Shelby's been around?"

"They came to my office yesterday. It didn't exactly go well."

Lorna grins. "You two always were like oil and water."

Kasey laughs. "Yeah, it didn't take him long to throw a tantrum and run out in a huff."

Lorna mulls that over as she finishes her drink. When it's empty, she sets the tumbler on the counter and leans forward. "But did you get a load of his tush as he walked away?" She wags her eyebrows at us. "That boy has grown up to be quite a man. I'd happily oil him up for a fight."

I gape at my stepmother, setting my glass next to hers. "I think I'm gonna need more of that moonshine."

Hashtag

THE LAST TWENTY-FOUR hours have ticked by slowly with no news from Kasey, and radio silence from Shelby, though the latter is deserving for the way our last conversation went. I was right to be angry after everything she's done, but I should've kept my emotions in check. Hayden's life is hanging in the balance, and yelling at her mother for our past isn't going to bring her back.

After my chat with Judge, the tunnel vision I had over Shelby's betrayal faded away, allowing me to focus only on Hayden. I just have to keep it that way.

For what feels like the hundredth time, I try to locate Hayden's phone, and for the hundredth time, I get nothing. My head falls into my hands. Nearly a day without sleep is wearing on me. She's still out there—I *know* she is. Of all the shit things in my life, whatever higher power is out there wouldn't take her from me. I have to find her before it's too late. And until I've found her, fuck sleep.

Brushing the weariness from my face, I try again. This time, my screen lights up like the Fourth of July. Fucking bingo! My eyes lock onto the area where her phone is currently active. Austin. She's here in Austin, not far from a newer strip mall downtown. I push out of my chair and grab my keys before walking out the door.

"Judge!" I yell out.

He steps outside one of the small meeting rooms, with GP and Twat Knot flanking him. "Got something?"

"Yeah. Downtown. Her cell phone's active."

"Go," he orders. "Take these two with you."

GP and TK look to each other with a nod.

"We're in, man."

"You lead, we'll follow."

The three of us head out the back door where a row of bikes are lined up behind the clubhouse. I pull my phone and wireless earbuds from my pocket. Putting the earbuds in place, I punch in the address for the strip mall near where her phone pinged a tower, and the directions pop up. I mount my bike, as does GP and Twat Knot, and we ride out of the parking lot toward our destination.

The ride takes roughly fifteen minutes with the construction traffic downtown, and the strip mall comes into view on our left. I find a secluded spot near the far-left side of the buildings and pull off. As I dismount my bike, I scan the area and groups of people milling about. This isn't going to be easy. Hayden could be anywhere in this crowd.

"What's the plan?" GP asks.

"Take her picture." Pulling an image I'd taken from Shelby's stack out of my back pocket, I hand it over to them. "You two check the businesses, ask the employees if they've seen her. I'm going to try to track down her phone signal."

"Sounds good." GP and Twat Knot disappear toward the businesses. Watching until they enter the first retail shop, I take my phone from my pocket and pull up the site. It pings again after I enter her number. Still active, and still here.

I consider my options carefully. I could try calling or texting her phone, but if she isn't in possession of it, it could spook whoever does have it into bolting, taking this opportunity with them. One wrong move and it's over until if, and when, Kasey can get the records from the game developer.

My phone rings.

"Hello?"

"We may have something," Twat Knot declares. "Gamer shop near the middle of the mall. Owner says he's seen Hayden in the last couple of weeks for some gaming competition he was running."

"On my way." My feet pound the pavement hard until I reach the store. Once Inside, I quickly scan the room. The shelves on the walls are stocked full of comic books, gaming systems, and pop culture merchandise. A wet dream for any kid at her age. Hell, if I wasn't hunting her down, I'd love nothing more than to bring her to a place like this.

Near the back corner is a group of computers placed in a square. A young boy sits alone, typing away on the keyboard, while a man lingers nearby, flipping through some comics. I find the guys standing off in the corner, talking with an older man. I stalk toward them.

"You've seen her?" I blurt out.

"Yes. She's one of the more regular customers I have. She and her mom come in every couple of weeks. Good kid."

Dammit, Shelby. You've brought her to Austin, knowing exactly where I live, yet you couldn't be bothered to introduce me to my kid? Judge's advice from earlier echoes inside of my head, bringing me back to reality. *Shut that shit down. Focus on Hayden, not her mother.*

"How long has it been since you last saw her?"

"Her mom brought her here for a BloxWorld National

Tournament qualifier over the weekend. She placed in the top ten nationally. She was really happy when she left," the older man adds. "Did something happen to her?"

"She's been missing for a few days."

"I'm so sorry to hear that. She's a sweet kid. I wish I knew more to help you." The shop owner's face falls into a worrisome look. "You guys private detectives or something?" He eyes the patch on my chest.

"Something like that," GP grumbles. "We just want to find her, so any other information you can think of, we'd really appreciate it."

"Were there other kids here playing in the tournament?" Twat Knot asks.

"Yes. In fact…" Pivoting on his heels, he looks in the area where the computers I noticed are set up. The man perusing the comics takes one look at us and heads straight for the door, but the kid's still there. "That young man over there played in the last tournament."

"Thanks," I mutter, snatching the photo from the old man's hand as I walk toward the kid. He notices me when I get close, and quickly exits out of his screen. Typical kid move, hiding what they're not supposed to be looking at from their parents. Suspicious, but not unheard of. He starts to shove a few things into his backpack when I reach him.

I shove the photo in front of his face. "You see this

girl before?" He pretends to study it, but recognition is clear on his face. He's seen her before.

"N—No…" he stutters nervously. I push the image closer, but he looks away, practically staring a hole through the floor. Bingo. Junior here has definitely seen her.

"She's my daughter," I offer up to see how he reacts. "Someone's taken her. You know anything about that?"

"I don't know her." This time, his voice is more panicked.

"You sure about that, kid?"

"Yeah, mister, I've never seen her before. Look, my dad's waiting for me outside. I really need to leave." The kid turns away from me and starts to pack his bag again. He's in a hurry to leave, but I don't think he has anyone waiting for him. On a hunch, I pull out my phone and punch in Hayden's number. A vibration inside his bag starts the second my call connects.

He turns around in horror when he realizes I have a phone in my hand. Before he can move, I snatch his bag from his hands and start digging inside. Karma and GP run toward me, blocking him from leaving. In the front pocket, I find the vibrating phone—Hayden's phone. The kid's face pales.

"Don't know my kid, huh? Where's my daughter?"

"Please, don't hurt me." His hands cover his face, thinking we're going to pound some sense into him.

"I'm not going to ask you again, kid."

"I don't know her," he bellows.

"How'd you get her phone?"

"I found it!" he cries. "A few blocks away, near the park."

Convenient story, but conviction flashes across his face. He's telling me the truth. Or, at least, believes he is.

"I'm going to need more information than that. Where specifically did you find it?"

The kid's body quivers in fear from being flanked by the three of us. "In a pink backpack by the dumpster."

"You want to take him with us, Hash?"

I consider it, but the kid can't be more than sixteen. The last thing the club needs is some Karen of a mother slapping us with a kidnapping charge for what we're doing now. We have to let him go. Catching a charge isn't an option.

"No. Cut him loose."

The kid pushes through Twat Knot and GP, running straight out the door. GP shoots a look over at me.

"You're just letting him go?"

"I am. We have her phone. We'll check out where he said he found it and see where it leads us."

"And if he lied to you?"

Shifting the phone down, I reveal the ID card I took. "I snagged this out of his bag. We got his name, photo, and address. Tracking him down won't be hard."

Twat Knot smiles. "Sneaky, man. I like it."

"What's next?"

"Let's head down to the park. We'll look for her bag."

I wave to the owner as we leave, but the look on his face tells me the second we step out the door, he's picking up the phone and reporting us to the police for talking to that kid the way we did. Just what we need, the fuzz up our ass. But hey, I could be wrong.

We make tracks toward our bikes, just as the familiar sound of sirens sound in the distance. I guess I wasn't wrong. I hate it when I'm right sometimes.

"You two lead the police on a wild goose chase. I'm going to head down to that park to check it out. Call Judge and let him know the situation."

"You got it, Hash."

The two of them take off south, away from the strip mall, when a cruiser comes speeding around the corner, taking off after them. The coast is clear. Firing up my bike, I head north, around the back of the strip mall toward the only park in the area I know is still down here —Garfield Park.

It only takes me five minutes before I reach the parking area near the side entrance of the park. At this time of day, it's filled with kids running around the playground while their nannies, or parents, sit glued to their phones on one of the nearby benches. A little girl with dark pigtails comes zooming by me as I walk down the sidewalk.

"'Cuse me," she giggles.

I wonder what Hayden was like at her age. The thought makes me realize how much of her life I've missed, like her birth, her first steps, first words, first day at school. All of her firsts. Things I never knew I missed, and now so desperately wish I'd been there to witness. I can never get that time back.

A big blue rubber ball goes flying through the air, nearly missing my nose, landing near a large trash barrel on the other side of the walkway. Two little boys freeze when I look over to them. I stalk over to retrieve their ball when something pink peeking out from behind it catches my eye. Could it be? I quicken my pace and charge toward the barrel, finding a bright pink backpack with *Hayden* stitched across the front of it.

The kid wasn't lying. Clutching the bag, I unzip it with shaking hands. Inside, I find a couple of notebooks, a set of keys, and a little black wallet with Iron Man's logo stitched along the side of it. My stomach drops. There's nothing that'll point me in the direction of where to find her.

Fuck. Another dead end. She'd been here. Or, at least, near here. How had no one seen anything? Everyone has their cameras out these days to capture every single moment on their cell phones. How did they miss this?

Cameras. That's it! I spin around, looking at all the businesses nearby. They'll have cameras. One of them may have been able to capture Hayden's abduction. Pulling my cell phone out of my pocket, I pull up GP in my contacts and hit his number.

He answers on the first ring. "Yeah?"

"You lose the cops?"

"We did. Pulled into a big parking garage and hid behind some box trucks. What's up?"

"Meet me at Garfield Park. I think I may have found a way to see when she was taken."

Chapter 15

Shelby

I SHOVE my way through the front door of the clubhouse, my anxiety clawing its way up my throat. "Where is she?" I ask when Wyatt comes into view.

"I don't know yet." He skirts around the table, moving through the group of very large, leather-clad men. "I found this, though." There, dangling from his finger, is Hayden's pink backpack.

I gape at it, looking it over, internally pleading for it to tell me where my baby girl is. "Where did you find that?"

He drops the bag at his feet. "Garfield Park. I also found her cell phone."

For a split second, the panic I've felt since Wyatt had texted me, telling me to meet him here, is replaced with hope. "That's a good thing, right?"

Wyatt presses his lips together, worry creasing his handsome face. "I don't know, Shel. I've been trying to locate her phone all along, but it was always off, or the battery was dead. But today it worked. I tracked it down to a comic book store in Austin. There was a kid there—a boy—who had her phone, saying he found it at Garfield Park. You neglected to mention the tournament Hayden was in not long ago."

The accusation is more in his words than his tone. I glare at him, forgetting the men surrounding us. "I didn't think it was important. Hayden is always online. What does the tournament have to do with anything?"

Wyatt throws his hands up in the air. "Jesus, Shelby! Everything is fucking important right now. The tournament might not play any part in this at all, but I find it pretty damn suspicious I found her phone with a kid from that same tournament, in the same place it was held, don't you?"

A lump forms in my throat when I realize I may have had a clue to where Hayden's been all along, but was too stupid to see it. "I'm sorry," I whisper, tears racing down my cheeks. "I take her to that store all the time."

Wyatt's head drops forward and he exhales what I can only assume is a cleansing breath. While he attempts to get himself under control, I once again become aware of the mountain of muscle all around me, their eyes focused on Wyatt and I. My cheeks feel like they're on fire. "Can we do this in private?"

Raising his head, he meets my gaze, his brows still furrowed in frustration. "No, we can't. This is a family matter, and whether you like it or not, Hayden is my family, and so is every one of the men in this room."

My emotions are all over the map, swirling and spinning inside of me like a hurricane, making it nearly impossible to know what to think or feel.

"There were three businesses with video cameras around the perimeter of Garfield Park," he says, no longer just addressing me.

I watch as he walks to the front of the room, and for the first time, I notice his computer, and a long cord running to the big screen television they have mounted on the wall. "The convenience store had a camera up that pointed to the sidewalk out front, but apparently, it hasn't worked in years." Reaching down, he clicks on a few keys, and I watch the television where his screen is mirrored. A tiny arrow moves this way and that as he clicks on things so fast, I can barely read each item before it's gone. "The liquor store had a camera that only shows a small portion of the road and sidewalk. They emailed me a copy of their footage. I've already scrolled through hours of it, starting with the day Hayden disappeared, but

I didn't see anything that had to do with the Kevin kid, nor her."

The arrow on the screen moves one last time, and a video window pops up, a play button and counter running along the bottom. "The last bit of footage took some finessing to get. The bank has four different cameras set up on the outside of their building. Two of them face the street."

Suddenly, there's my baby on the screen. Her pink backpack is strapped over her shoulders as she walks along the sidewalk. Her long, dark hair is tucked behind her ear as she looks down at her phone. The video is grainy, and you can't make out her features, but there's no doubt in my mind that it's Hayden.

"I almost gave up," Wyatt says, walking to the front of the room as the rest of us watch the footage. "So many hours of video, each one boring as fuck. And then I see this."

The room is silent as we watch the soundless video. Hayden walks a little farther, her tiny frame almost out of the picture when she comes to a stop. My heart races as she looks up and appears to say something. *Who is she talking to?*

A young boy appears. I don't recognize him, but Hayden seems to. Maybe it's a boy from school? Camp? The pair have only been speaking for a few moments when a rusted white van pulls up. The side door opens, and Hayden's pulled inside. I watch in horror as the young boy jumps inside and slams the door closed before it speeds away. It all happens so fast. One minute she's there, talking to a boy, and the next, she's gone. Both of them are just... gone.

"You recognize that kid?" Wyatt asks.

I shake my head, assuming he's talking to me. "I've never seen that kid before in my life."

"That was the fucking kid who had her phone," GP snarls from beside me.

"And the kid who lied to my face when I asked him about Hayden. We need to find this fucking kid. And once I've found Hayden, I'm gonna kill him."

Hashtag

THE KID IS the key to this whole fucking thing, I know it. The security footage proves his involvement without a doubt. He's the missing link in finding my daughter.

Judge walks into the room, just as I slide the ID from my pocket and lean it against the top of the keyboard.

"Heard about the video. What can I do to help?" His eyes go straight to the ID. "Who do we have here?"

"Snagged it off the kid from earlier, the one *in* the video."

"Good work," Judge declares, squeezing my shoulder.

"You stole the kid's ID?" Shelby asks. "How did you do it without him seeing it?"

"The kid was too busy pissing his pants when Hayden's phone rang, he didn't even notice."

"Do you think he knows where she is?" Her big brown eyes are filled with hope and anger.

"Mr. Kevin Tucker here knows who has our daughter. And we just watched Hayden be forced into that van. He was involved in her kidnapping." I type in his full name and the address from the card into my favorite search engine before picking it up and showing it to Shelby. "This is our insurance policy."

"He's a kid, Wyatt." I can see the uncertainty on her face. A mother never wants to see harm come to any child. But a mother would also rain down hell to find her own child if they're in danger.

"A kid who watched our daughter get thrown into a van against her will and did absolutely nothing to stop it. He's not innocent."

"He's still a kid," she cries. "Maybe he can help us. Maybe he's innocent."

Innocent? "Let's just see what he has to say when we roll up to his house."

Shelby looks down at her hands, picking at her fingernails. "Do you think you'll have to hurt him?"

"I honestly don't know, Shel. This boy isn't just some kid, as you keep saying. He lost the right to play the kid card when he lied to me about how he got her phone." She nods, but doesn't look up from her fingers.

"Do what you have to do." She crosses her arms tightly against her chest, and it takes a hero's effort not to glance down at her ample cleavage. *Jesus, Hash. This is not the time.*

"We're gonna find her, Shel. And it's not like we're going into this kid's house, guns blazing. We aren't heartless bastards. We won't hurt him unless we have to."

Shelby mulls that over before finally nodding.

My computer beeps from behind me. "Got something," I declare as the screen pops up with a list of results from the search. With a click of the mouse, I switch over to the maps function. No street view. Pulling up another window, I type in the address on a realtor site. Nothing. We'll have to go in blind.

"Fuck, is that Martinsville?" Judge presses a finger to the screen. Shit, he's right. The kid lives on the outskirts of Martinsville, one of the most dangerous neighborhoods in the city.

"Why is Martinsville bad?" Shelby asks at nearly a whisper.

Back before the recession, it was the heart of manufacturing in Austin. When the market tanked, all the factories closed up shop or moved overseas, leaving the people who depended on them in the area jobless, and some homeless. Things had only gotten worse as the years went on, with violence and trafficking moving in as the factories moved out. The club had been trying for years to help stop the routes these guys used to move women in and out, but never had much luck. Without an in, anything we did went nowhere. Now my daughter could be in the thick of it.

The look on Judge's face confirms what I already know is true. Martinsville is known for trafficking young girls. Hayden was taken for a purpose. Trafficking always needs younger, fresher blood, and she ticks off the checklist. She may not have even realized they were grooming her to be taken until it was too late.

The last bit causes bile to rise up my throat. Trafficking rings move girls around like pawns on a chess board. She may not even be there anymore. We have to move fast.

Ignoring the fear on Shelby's face, I attempt to remain professional about the whole shitty situation. "How do you want to do this, Judge? Getting in there unnoticed isn't going to be easy."

He considers our options. "We need to get eyes on this place without drawing attention."

Chewing on my lower lip, an idea pops into my head. "Why don't we send Priest in one of the club girls' cars?"

Shelby stands there silently, watching us lay out a

potential battle plan. Her eyes fall to the ground and stay there. She's scared.

"It's risky. If it's a big operation, they'll have eyes out. "

"Single guy driving through the thick of Martinsville looking to score won't draw any attention."

"That's true," Judge hesitantly agrees. "I'll get Missy to loan him her Grand Am. He'll slip in, get eyes on the place, and report back. We'll take a couple of the work trucks and follow him, and we'll decide from there how we want to play it. I'll get the ball rolling. Wheels moving in fifteen." Judge stalks out of the room, leaving Shelby and I alone.

I push out of my chair and stand next to her. Everything inside of me wants to reach out and embrace her. I know she's scared. Fuck, I am too, but we have to stay strong for our daughter. Falling apart when we're this close isn't going to bring her back any faster.

"Do you think she's really there?"

"I don't know if she is or isn't, but this kid..." Snagging the ID from my keyboard, I show it to her again before slipping it back into my pocket. "He's the last person we know of who saw her. We find him, we get our best shot at finding her."

Shelby places her hand on my arm and locks her gaze

on mine. "I saw the way you looked at Judge. What aren't you telling me?"

She deserves to know of my suspicions of why Hayden was taken, but that knowledge comes with an entirely new set of heartbreak. With a sigh, I make my decision.

"The last few years, there's been a route of human trafficking going right through Martinsville. The club has tried to cut it off, but they always start right back up again." The words taste foul on my tongue.

"Oh my God, Wyatt. You don't think...?"

"I don't know. But honestly, the way she was taken, and knowing where that asshole kid is from, it's not a possibility we can rule out."

"No, not my daughter. It's not possible. I refuse to believe that!"

"I don't want to consider it either, but everything points in that direction. The sooner we find her, the better. Traffickers usually stash the girls for a few days before moving them out. There's still time."

"What if we... don't?" she sobs, a line of glistening tears streaming down her face. I reach out my hand, and with a gentle swipe, wipe them from her face. Her skin feels so soft under my touch. She leans into my hand, allowing me to touch her for the first time since she came back.

"I promise you, come hell or high water, I will find her."

"Trucks are loaded up. Judge is ready to roll," Karma informs me from the door, and then disappears just as quickly as he arrived.

I turn back toward my desk and open the top drawer, retrieving my handgun from its resting place. Stowing it in the back of my jeans, I say, "I made you a promise, and I intend to keep it." I walk out of the room, leaving her there with the knowledge of the fate our daughter could be facing, and no means to anything herself. It eats at me with every step I take as I make my way outside.

I reach for the passenger side door when I notice GP's eyes trailing over to the door behind me. I turn to see what he's looking at, and find Shelby heading toward me.

"Where the hell do you think you're going?" I bark as she slips past me and opens the truck door.

"With you."

"The fuck you are. You need to stay here where it's safe," I fire back, closing the door on her.

"I don't care what you think. I'm going in this truck or following behind you in my car. Your call." You have got to be shitting me right now. We have no idea what we're walking in to. Fuck. Judge is going to have my ass later for this, but I'm left here with little choice. We've got to get a move on.

"Get in," I growl, opening the door. GP scowls as Shelby jumps up and into the front cab, settling into the middle seat. Climbing in after her, I close the door.

"The fuck she doing here?" Stone Face complains from the back seat. "Ain't no place for a woman."

"Try telling her that," I respond. "Let's just go find this kid and get back before Judge realizes she's with us." I shift back into my seat as GP takes the truck out of park and heads south.

Martinsville is about a fifteen-minute drive without traffic, and tonight, it figures everyone's out on the fucking road. We barely make it a mile before we come to a full stop. GP stews behind the wheel.

Shelby's knee bounces anxiously next to mine. If she only knew the fury swirling around inside of me. One of my foster fathers used to tell me that I was like a duck on a pond. On the surface, it seemed as if I was still and calm, though under it, I was a raging storm of feet, kicking and fighting to stay afloat. It wasn't until today that I understand what he meant. Compared to Shelby, my demure is even keel.

It takes another forty minutes before we finally make it to the right exit. As we do, my cell phone rings.

"Yeah."

"Priest called. He made it to the address," Judge declares.

"What's the situation?"

"Place is burned to the ground, and still smoking. I'm sorry, Hash, but there's nothing left there."

My fingers pinch the bridge of my nose. *Fuck*. And just like that, we're back to square one, and no closer to finding Hayden.

Shelby

"WHAT NOW?" I ask, tamping down my fear as I follow Wyatt down the hall and into his room.

"I don't fucking know!" he shouts, his hands flying up as he whirls around to face me. "I don't fucking know what to do here. I'm off my game. You might not know this, Shelby, but finding people is kind of my thing. I can find anyone online, but I can't find my own fucking kid."

His frustration does nothing to make me feel better. In fact, it scares the holy hell out of me. I'd come to Wyatt because he was the only person on God's green earth I *knew* would find my baby girl. But he hasn't done that, and now it sounds like he's giving up.

"I'll pay you," I blurt out without thinking.

Wyatt's face twists with confusion. "What the fuck are you talking about?"

"I don't have much, but I can find the money. Whatever you need, I'll pay you. Just find my daughter." Tears pour down my cheeks like waterfalls as the panic I'm feeling builds. But Wyatt changes everything with his reply.

"Fuck you, Shelby. Fuck you. Fuck Kasey. Fuck your goddamn offer to pay me." I gape up at him as he places his nose a couple of inches from mine. "In case you've forgotten, Hayden is my fucking daughter too. I'm not some hired tech nerd you can pay to track her down. I'm her fucking father. Not that you've made it possible for me to have a relationship with her."

With every word he spews at me, I shrink farther and farther away. "I'll find Hayden, but not because you paid me. I'll find her because she's my fucking blood." He shakes his head in disbelief and steps back, his angry eyes looking me up and down. "Who have you become, Shel? You may look pretty much the same, but I don't even recognize you."

"You're right," I whisper, realizing the truth of those words as I speak them. "I've fucked it up. I ruined what you could have had with Hayden. But you aren't innocent in this, Wyatt." I straighten my spine and look him dead in the eyes, finally ready to confront him about the pain he'd caused me in this very room all those years ago.

"You chose being a slut over me. I thought we were going to be together forever. I thought we were going to be a family."

His eyes narrow. "What the fuck are you talking about, woman? You never gave me a goddamn chance to choose anything."

Heat washes over me as my anger reaches its breaking point. I shove past him and point toward the bed in the center of the room. "I'm talking about the night you were patched in! I'm talking about the two bimbos you had in that very bed, catching God knows how many diseases."

His eyebrows furrow. "What bimbos? What are you fucking saying?" He sounds so sincere, I almost believe him.

"I was here that night, Wyatt. I showed up to your little party and went looking for you. One of the guys told me which room was yours, and when I came down the hall, I saw you. I saw you fucking Sasha and Layla in this very room, in this bed." My body trembles with buried emotions. "You fucking broke us that night, you know. I was coming to tell you I was pregnant. I was so scared to tell you, and then..." I shake my head. "You just fucking broke us."

"I broke us?" he snarls. "I didn't fuck anybody that

night. Ask Judge. Ask GP. They'll all tell you the same fucking thing. I was going to propose to you that night, but you never showed up."

Before I can stop myself, I shove him with all my might. "You're lying! Stop fucking lying! You ruined everything. You ruined me!"

"Shelby," he intones, his voice softer now, more soothing. "I've never lied to you, not once since I met you back when we were kids. Whoever you saw in this bed wasn't me."

I search for the memory of that night and mentally blow off the cobwebs. It was so long ago now. Is he telling the truth? Was it someone else?

That bitch.

Sasha's back was to me as she rode the man lying on the bed. Layla was facing me, up near the headboard, riding his face. When she saw me, she looked pleased with herself.

I'd never actually seen the man's face, as she was on it. The only part of him I saw was his legs and feet. It could have been anyone.

"Layla and Sasha," I whisper. "They were in your bed, riding you."

"It wasn't me."

"Layla saw me. She made a show of it, smiling at me,

like I caught you cheating on me with them. She was happy about it."

"Shel, it wasn't me. The second I realized you weren't here, I went looking for you. I went to Kasey's, and even your dad's. Fucker gave me a shiner when I tried to go inside to find you."

I look into his eyes and see the sincerity in them. It wasn't him. I step away from him.

"Oh, God," I sob, clapping my hand over my mouth.

I'd abandoned him that night. I'd taken off and never looked back. I'd kept his daughter from him.

"Shelby," Wyatt calls, pulling me back to the present. "Please tell me you didn't keep my daughter a secret from me for all these years because of some fucked-up assumption you made."

I pull in a deep breath, hoping to keep the tears from falling. I've never cried as much as I have in the past few days. "I'm so sorry, Wyatt."

"You're sorry?" he screams. "You're fucking sorry? You left me! You fucking walked out on me without a word, all because of a fucking misunderstanding, and you're fucking sorry?"

Any hope I had of keeping my tears at bay disappear at the tone of his voice. His face is red, his eyes full of rage. Violent sobs rip from my throat.

Placing his hands on my arms, he gives me a gentle shake. "You destroyed me."

I don't know what else to say. "I'm sorry."

He presses his forehead to mine, his shaky breath fanning across my tear-soaked cheeks. "You fucking gutted me."

"I'm sorry."

"You left me." His lips barely graze mine, but that simple touch is like lighting a torch. The darkness of my mistake, and the pain of what I'd done, disappears in an instant.

I pop up on the tips of my toes and reach up, spearing my fingers into the short hairs at the back of his neck. My lips peck tentatively at his once, twice, and then a third time.

And that's all it takes. Before I know what's happening, my legs are wrapping around his waist, his hands gripping my ass, pulling me closer. Our kiss is fierce and hot, passionate and punishing, and it captures the breath from my lungs.

My heart races out of control as he walks me backward and toward the bed. My back hits the mattress with a soft bounce, and I can't look away as he whisks off his shirt.

The years have been kind to Wyatt. He's thicker, more muscular and toned. His face is more manly, yet somehow more handsome than when we were kids. He's even better than what I remember.

"Take off your pants, Shel," he orders, his voice husky.

Lifting my ass, I wiggle out of my skinny jeans, my gaze never leaving his as he strips out of his own pants. Just as I'm about to peel off my shirt, I pause.

The last time Wyatt had seen me naked, I was so young. Since then, I've had a kid of my own. I have stretch marks, and my breasts aren't nearly as perky as they used to be. *What the hell are we doing?*

I need to call this whole thing off. It's stupid. We shouldn't be doing this. "Wyatt..."

His face twists in anger as his hands shoot out to grasp the hem of my shirt. "Take it off."

"No, this isn't—"

"I need you, Shel. I need you so fucking bad."

That's all I need to hear, because fuck me, I need him too.

Lifting my arms, I hold his gaze as he pulls my shirt up and over my head. He takes me in before leaning forward, staring directly into my eyes as he presses a kiss to one nipple, and then the other.

He stands back, and I see his cock ready for me. I want it more than I've ever wanted anything.

"You're still so fucking gorgeous, Shel. That hasn't changed."

I moan, rolling my hips when he drags a finger through my center, collecting the moisture and placing it in his mouth. His eyes fall closed. "God, I've missed the way you taste."

Need claws at me from the inside out. I need him inside of me. I need him to fill me. I need to feel at one with him.

"Please, Wyatt," I beg.

"All these years," he says, crawling lower, his face just inches from my sex. "All these years, I've been with different women, but not one of them have ever mattered." He kisses my clit once, twice, and then thrusts his tongue out, pressing hard, dragging it along my slit, hitting every nerve.

I can hardly breathe. Frozen, I pop up onto my elbows and watch every movement he makes.

"They never mattered because they weren't you. This pussy here?" He sucks my clit, flicking his tongue back and forth, sending lightning bolts of pleasure throughout my body. "This pussy owns me. Always has, always will."

I moan, grinding my hips against his face. I can't tear my eyes away as he licks and sucks, driving me closer to the edge than I've ever been before.

"Please," I beg.

"So good." Burying his face deeper, his tongue moves faster.

My release hits me like a ton of bricks, coming on hard and fast, making me tremble with pleasure.

"God, Wyatt," I gasp.

His tongue begins to slow. Though my release was incredible, I need him to fill me.

Grabbing his face, I pull it away from my pussy, my wetness glistening along his lips and chin. It's honestly the sexiest fucking thing I've ever seen. Swiping my thumb across his moistened lips, I lock eyes with him, demanding, "Fuck me."

He grins. "What the lady wants, the lady gets."

The bed wobbles a little as he climbs up over me, positioning himself at my entrance. It's been so long. So many wasted years. I've missed this. I've missed him.

His nostrils flare as he looks into my eyes, and without a doubt, I know he's missed it too. "You ready?"

I nod, more ready for this than I've been for anything. "I need you."

With his eyes gazing intently into mine, he begins to fill me, slowly. It's everything, and so much more.

I glide my fingertips over his muscular back, allowing myself to feel every inch of him. Goose bumps race along his skin as I drag my nails across it, and I can't help but revel in the fact that after all these years, I can still do that to him.

Our kisses grow long and deep as he thrusts harder, faster. I move my hips in rhythm with his, like a dancer moving to the beat of a favorite song. Moans of pleasure echo off the walls, surrounding us as we grind into each other.

My head spins as I near my release for a second time. My breaths become choppy, and I come, basking in the pleasure.

Wyatt groans softly, holding me to him as he releases, giving me what used to be mine. What should have always been mine.

He holds himself above me, his lips grazing the tip of my nose, my brow, and finally my lips.

As our heartbeats slowly level out, I don't move a muscle. As much as I'm enjoying being in the arms of the only man I've ever loved, I can't help but wonder: what now?

The question plays over and over in my mind for the hundredth time when my cell phone chimes.

Wyatt drops his head and groans, rolling to his side. My heart warms a little when he doesn't pull away completely. He leaves a hand on my waist as I lean to the side to reach for my phone.

"It's from Kasey," I say, using my thumb to unlock the screen.

Kasey: Blox World files are in. I've forwarded them to your email so you can get started, but also have hard copies here at the office. If you need them, I can deliver them tomorrow.

I lift my gaze to meet Wyatt's, hope blooming in my heart. "We have the files."

Chapter 18

Hashtag

SHELBY STANDS, looking over my shoulder as I click the link Kasey sent to her phone. It takes me to a virtual cloud folder filled with subfolders, organized by date.

"There has to be hundreds," she murmurs.

"You ready for this?" A question I didn't know if I could answer honestly myself. Looking at her conversations is a necessary evil to help find her or her online friend. But knowing what could be lurking inside of them is bothering me more than I care to admit out loud. I've seen for myself the sadistic shit predators say and do to groom kids online with some of the work I've done for the club. Those fuckers deserve to rot in hell, and this guy would be getting a one-way ticket the second I found his ass. There'll be no running from what I have planned for him.

"We have to do this for her, Wyatt. Even if..." She trails off, tears glistening in her eyes. "What if she sent him things?"

"We'll deal with it together, Shelby, and when we get her home."

"You mean *if* we get her home."

"*When* we get her home, we'll be having our first family meeting about internet safety while I install every type of tracking software known to man on her and her electronics for the rest of her life."

Shelby tries to smile, but it doesn't reach her eyes.

With a deep sigh, I dive in and click on the first folder, dated nearly a year ago.

P4r4D0X: Cool castle.

P4r4D0X: Do you like mine?

P4r4D0X: Hello?

A conversation that went without a reply. The next few are similar messages that again show no replies from Hayden's username. Whoever was sitting on the other side of the screen clearly wasn't getting the hint that she didn't want to chat. If he was looking for an easy mark, he'd have moved on quickly to someone interested in chatting with him. The fact that he hadn't given up after so many weeks of silence is surprising, which begs the question: what changed? I find my answer a few more folders down, dated six months ago.

P4r4D0X: You have a logic error in your coding.

HayDay: No, I don't.

P4r4D0X: The second level door won't open. I can fix it for you.

HayDay: No.

The fucker pointed out a flaw in her build, and she responded back. He knew what he was doing, no doubt about it. He waited and kept trying until he dangled bait to get her to respond, knowing that a serious coder wouldn't take lightly to someone questioning their skills.

"He baited her."

"He what?"

"Outwardly questioning someone's work is a huge insult in the coding community. He had to have watched her build and found, or maybe even created the error himself in order to open the door to talking to her."

"Why would he do that? With what you've mentioned about the game's safeguards, how would he have known he was talking to a teenager?"

"That's the million-dollar question. When did she start playing in the tournaments for Blox World?"

Her beautiful lips thin as she thinks. "The first one was a few months back... April, I think. Why? Do you think she may have met this guy at one? I always went with her."

"It's a possibility. But let's see what else we can find."

My attention goes back to the files. The next conversation between them, she initiates it, thanking him for pointing out the error she'd missed. From there, the conversations become more friendly and frequent. Almost all of them seem innocent enough: coding debates, critiques on each other's current world builds, and pop culture. From the outside, it seems normal enough for two kids talking, not the adult I suspect is on the other side of the screen. Nothing makes sense until I click open one of the more recent chat threads.

P4r4D0X: Can I have your number?

HayDay: How? The bots block that info.

P4r4D0X: It's easy. Watch. if (x == 5661365) See? The game just thinks we're sharing code.

HayDay: My mom wouldn't like it if I gave my number out.

"Damn right, I wouldn't," Shelby growls while I jot down the phone number to search later. "What was she thinking? Hayden knows better. Or, at least, I thought she did."

"She's a teenager. They make bad decisions all the time."

"How would you know?" she questions sarcastically.

"Because she has half my DNA."

She rolls her eyes at me, but we both know it's the truth. I may never have been a part of her life growing up, but she's my daughter. My blood is in her veins. Rebellious streaks are just a part of it.

"What does the next one say?"

Clicking on the file, I hit pay dirt.

P4r4D0X: Big tournament this week. You playing?

HayDay: No. My mom has to work.

P4r4D0X: Go on your own. I could meet you there.

HayDay: My mom would kill me.

P4r4D0X: If she's at work, how would she find out?

HayDay: I can't sneak out like that.

P4r4D0X: I want to meet you. Just take a bus. You can call me when you get there.

"That's a few days before she disappeared."

"Looks like her friend convinced her to bail and bus it down to Austin to meet him, and we know what happened when she got there."

Pulling from the notepad with the number on it, I exit out of the files and pop it into the location software I had used to ping Hayden's phone. Nothing comes up. I try to call it using a fake number online, but it never connects. Fuck. Another dead end.

"It's probably a burner phone." I spin to look at

Shelby, who shrugs. "What? I like crime shows. What's next?"

"With the kid in the wind, and this number being a dead end, we're stuck. Judge sent Priest and Burnt out to keep an eye on the place in Martinsville and the comic store for the kid."

"I hate not knowing, Wyatt. I wish she never started playing that stupid game. If I had put my foot down, none of this would have happened."

"Hindsight is a bitch. You could have never predicted she would go rogue like this."

"I hate that she's out there, alone and scared, while we're here playing this stupid game."

Shit. Playing the game. "Why didn't I think of that sooner?" Shoving out of my chair, I grab Hayden's laptop from my other desk, bringing it back with me and opening it up.

"Think of what sooner?"

"If he found Hayden playing this game, what's not to say that he's not still doing it under a new name? I could go create my own account and follow what Hayden did. Maybe he'll take notice and try to chat with me."

"Would that even work? What if he just bailed on it the second they had Hayden?"

"Because predators never get enough, and they always want more. And when something works, they'll keep doing it until their supply runs dry or they get caught."

Shelby stalks over to the other desk and wheels the chair over next to me.

"Let's play."

Chapter 19

Shelby

ONE THING THIS GAME PROVES, without a doubt, is that Hayden didn't get this particular interest from me. *Holy crap, this is boring.*

At first, I try watching the way Wyatt builds a world, digging things and developing others, but honestly, it looks like nothing more than a bunch of pixelated blocks to me, making my brain hurt.

Wyatt and I never were very similar, but when we were younger, that's what always made us special. He was into computers and classic rock, while I was into art and heavy metal. He loved quiet days spent online, and I loved nights out on the town.

His fingers fly at lightning speed. This man is the father of my child. The same man who stole my heart all those years ago. And when I ran, I'd left it with him.

There've been guys since him, but none of them lasted. There's never been anyone who could fill those giant motorcycle boots.

"I'm gonna go for a drive," I tell him, unable to sit here in this room for another moment. It still smells like sex, and I desperately need some time to wrap my head around the revelations made earlier tonight.

The clicking at the keyboard stops abruptly as he turns to me. "Everything okay?"

No, everything is not "okay." In fact, it's far from okay, but I can't get into that right now. I need to figure it out for myself. "Yeah. I just need some fresh air, and a chance to clear my head."

He narrows his eyes, studying me, before finally nodding. "You're coming back, right?"

"Of course. I won't be long." My words are casual, but inside, my gut is churning. I need to get out of here to think. I need to fucking breathe.

Reaching out, he snatches my hand as I pass, lifting it to his lips. When he presses a gentle kiss to the back of it, I melt a little right there on the floor. "Be careful."

I swallow past my swirling emotions and force a smile. "I will."

I hadn't realized how late it was, but outside, the birds are singing their morning song, and the sun's just barely peeking up on the horizon. It's not until I climb into my car and turn on the engine that I see it's nearly five o'clock in the morning. No wonder I feel tired.

I pull out of the parking lot and onto the deserted road. There's no traffic at this time of morning, and with all the distractions swirling around inside my head, that's definitely a good thing.

It wasn't him.

That's the thought I can't put out of my head. All these years, I've cut him out of our lives because I thought he'd betrayed me, and it wasn't even him!

What kind of person does that make me? I reacted first, never bothering to ask questions. I just packed up and ran. I've struggled all these years as a single mom and kept Hayden to myself, never offering her a chance to even get to know her father. How will they forgive me? How will *I* forgive myself?

And Hayden. How is it possible to be both angry with someone and need them so damn much? I can't believe she got caught up in this. I can't believe she arranged to meet someone online, whether she thought he was a kid or not. She knows better than that. I may not know much about computers, but I began cautioning her at a young age about internet safety.

She always paid attention, followed the rules, and used her head. Until now.

A burnt-out house comes into view and I stop in front

of it, staring at the remains. I hadn't meant to drive this far. I hadn't even consciously come here, but I think part of me needed to see it.

Was Hayden kept here? Does the kid who used to live here know where she is? Why did it burn down?

That last part worries me more than the rest. It shows aggression and recklessness by the people who have her. It shows they weren't attached to their own home, let alone Hayden. They wouldn't hesitate to hurt her if they had to.

A knuckle taps against the glass of my driver's side window, snapping me to attention. I don't know the man outside my car, but I recognize him. He's a member of the Black Hoods, and he's huge. I look down and read the name on his cut: Priest.

"You need to leave," he orders through the glass.

"Are you following me?" I ask incredulously, not lowering the window.

He only responds with, "It's not safe here. You need to leave, now."

I glare at him, but it doesn't seem to faze him. Instead, he turns and walks away, disappearing around the corner.

I take one last, long look at the house before pulling away from the curb, leaving my unanswered questions buried in the soot. I'm less than a block away when the motorcycles pull up behind me. Priest and another guy from the club aren't even trying to hide.

I turn down a side street to test my theory, and sure enough, they turn too. *Motherfucker.*

Using the hands-free feature on the car's dash, I call Wyatt.

"Yeah?"

"Do you care to explain why two very large men on motorcycles are following me all over hell's half acre?"

He sighs. "You shouldn't be there, Shelby. The whole town isn't safe, and these fuckers know we're onto them."

In theory, I understand what he's saying, but that doesn't answer my direct question. "Why do you have them following me?"

"Are you listening to me?"

I slam my fist down on the dash. "Damnit, Wyatt! Why are they following me?"

"Because you're mine!" he shouts. "And because you're putting yourself in danger. It was a stupid fucking move, so I want to make sure you're safe."

You're mine. Those two words extinguish my anger the minute he speaks them. Does he mean that? Does he still want me? After everything I've done to him and Hayden by keeping them apart, does he truly still want me?

"Shelby?" he urges, his voice softer.

"Yeah?"

"Come home, baby. Just… come home."

Warmth washes over me. *Mine. Baby. Home.* "Okay."

I'm still pissed, but now I'm pissed remembering just what it was about Wyatt that made me fall in love with him in the first place.

Hashtag

I HAVE no idea what Shelby was thinking going back to that house, let alone to Martinsville, on her own. I know she needed to get out of her own head and worries for a while, but her decision put her in danger. Had Priest and Burnt not been keeping tabs on the place for the kid at Judge's request, I could have lost her too. Once was enough. I'm not prepared for it to happen again.

I wait anxiously outside the clubhouse for a glimpse of her car to pull into the parking lot when Karma walks by and takes notice. He shifts direction, grinning his stupid fucking grin as he approaches me.

"You look like someone shit in your cereal. What did Shelby do now?"

"Priest found her driving by the Martinsville house."

Karma busts out in a hearty laugh, and I sneer.

"Shit hasn't changed one bit with her. When you say zig, she zags."

"You're not kidding. I don't know what got into her."

He smiles. "You did, and now there's two of you. The world will never be the same again."

Shelby's car pulls into the parking lot at last, and relief washes over me. Her purple hair peeks out from the open door, but it's her face I notice first, and she's pissed. Great.

"Go easy on her, man. But if you don't, I have fifty on her in the first round."

Karma walks off just as Shelby gets to me. I raise my hand up to stop her from unleashing on me outside. We don't need an audience for what I have to say to her. I lower my hand, grab hers, and drag her along behind me until we reach my room and close the door.

"You're having me followed," she snarls. *Ding. Ding. Round one.*

"No. Judge put the prospects on the house." That's the truth. When they spotted her driving by the house, I had them tail her for her own protection. "Why the fuck did you go there? You know Martinsville isn't safe, yet there you were."

She paces the floor in front of me. "I couldn't just sit here anymore and watch you play games. We're getting nowhere fast, and every second we're not out there looking for her, we're losing out on our chance of finding her."

"Is that what you think? That I'm just sitting here playing games? I'm doing what I can to attract the people who've taken our daughter. I've gone without sleep, trying to bait them into contacting me. Outside of finding that kid, which is like looking for a needle in a fucking haystack, this is our lead now. Judge has our guys watching every single place this kid might go."

"I can't just sit here and do nothing. Hayden's out there, scared, and I can't do a damn thing to help her."

"Then let me do it. Let me take on your worries and your burdens. We can't find her if you and I are on opposite pages. We have to be a united front—a family."

"There's that word again—*family*." She says it like it's the dirtiest word in the English language.

"We are a family, Shelby. There's no going back. I won't live my life without my daughter being a part of it. Hayden isn't going to go back to living without a father again, and I want you to be a part of that."

All the anger and fear drains from her and she stops, her eyes filling with hope. "After everything I've done, you still want us to be a family?"

"Jesus, Shelby, I've always fucking loved you. How can you not see that?"

"No, you can't love me, not after I left, and not after Hayden," she sobs.

Hayden. Yeah, that part makes it a lot harder. "Tell me about her. I want to know everything."

Her face is still wet with tears, but one side of her mouth tips up. "She's amazing, Wyatt. She's beautiful and brilliant, and so fucking fearless. She loves people, and has always been the kid who make friends with everyone. Even the outcasts."

"Sounds like you."

She grins. "I've always thought she has the best of both of us."

The best of both of us. I like that.

"Shel, I'm not gonna lie. I hate what you did and why you did it. I hate everything that resulted from all of it. But…" Reaching up, I cup my hands around her face to stop her from pacing. A beautiful face. "You're it for me. Always have been, and always will be. I've spent years hating you, but at the same time, waiting for you to walk back through that door. There's no way in hell I'm gonna let you walk away again."

"How will we ever get past this, though? The hurt. The anger. There's no way we can be together. Not after what I've done."

"We have to be," I tell her. "Because I swear to God, my heart has been in pieces since the day you left, and I didn't even know it. Now you're here, and it's like every single day, even when you're being a total asshole, you stitch another piece back together."

Her lips twitch. "You saying I'm an asshole?"

I shrug. "Maybe some of the time."

She grins at me for a moment, and I can't help but think of how much I've missed being the one to make those lips grin like that.

"We have a lot to talk about," she warns.

"We do. And we will. We have time."

Her big doe eyes stare back at me, and I can't take it anymore. This time, when we kiss, there's no anger. There's no tension. There's just love.

Her lips are like the softest silk, and in that moment, it's like no time has passed. Once again, I'm that young, headstrong, wannabe biker, and she's that punky, spunky teenage girl with hopes of forever with the boy she loves. In that moment, our lost time is forgotten.

I kiss her deeper, reveling in the taste, sound, and feel of the woman I've always loved. Slowly, I walk her back, stopping when her legs hit the bed. Pulling me closer, I lower her back to the mattress, never breaking our connection.

We're caught in the moment of tongues, hands, and hot breath. Our mouths explore places we haven't been in years. I cup her breast, my thumb sliding back and forth across her nipple as we move. Our hips roll as one, locked together like magnets. Every touch of her hand stitches up another piece of my heart.

"I love you so fucking much," I whisper into her ear.

"I love you," she gasps.

"You're not leaving me again."

"Never."

"You're fucking mine, Shel."

I feel her tighten around me. "I've always been yours."

She feels so perfect. So right. So mine. "Come for me, baby."

Her release was so close, but those words are all it takes to send her off into oblivion. I watch her face as she moans long and low, her walls clutching my cock like a vice. Her fingernails dig into my back, and I can't hold off any longer.

I come long and hard. Starbursts go off behind my eyelids, while jolts of electric pleasure shoot up and down my spine.

Shelby lies silently in my arms as our chests heave in the aftermath. Her damp skin pressing so tightly against mine is the closest feeling to heaven I've ever felt. Sleeping together before had been satisfying a primal urge, but this is so much more. It's an apologetic dance of

our pasts, and a promise of something more in the future
—our future.

A soft snore escapes her lips as she drifts off to sleep.
I take my opportunity to slip from the bed, leaving her
there to rest. As much as I'd like to sleep beside her,
there's still work to be done. Finding my boxers on the
floor, I pull them up over my hips, just as a ding from my
computer echoes into the room.

I march over to the desk and click the mouse. A chat
request box blinks on the toolbar from Blox World. I
select it, and literally feel my heart stop as I read the
message.

HayDay911: H needs your help. Can we meet?

I shake as I type out my response.

GamerGirl13: Yes. When?

HayDay911: Today. I'll come to you.

I start to answer the user back, but they log off.

I think we may have just found that fucking haystack
needle after all.

Chapter 21

Shelby

"YOU CAN'T KEEP me prisoner in here, Wyatt."

He sighs, his head falling back in frustration. "Jesus Christ, woman. I'm not keeping you prisoner. I'm keeping you safe until I know what this asshole wants."

I glare at his retreating back with my arms crossed, looking like a petulant child, but I don't care. I want to know who this HayDay911 is. I want to know what he knows about Hayden.

A shout from outside wafts through the window, and I forget all about Wyatt as I turn and run to look. At first, all I see is a wall of men. It seems like every single member of the club is there, forming a barricade between whoever's standing out front and the clubhouse.

I see Judge and Wyatt through the spaces between them, talking to someone, but I can't see who.

And then, the men part, each of them turning toward the clubhouse, but waiting for Wyatt to pass. And beside him is the kid who'd had Hayden's phone.

Oh, hell no. I'm not hiding in here like some china doll, knowing this kid could lead me to my daughter.

I whip open the door to Wyatt's room and hurry toward the common area, getting there just as Wyatt places a cold bottle of water on the table in front of him.

"Goddamnit, Shelby," Wyatt snaps when he sees me.

A couple of the guys chuckle, but I pay them no mind. Instead, I focus on the kid. "Where's my daughter?"

He looks up at me, and that's when I notice his face. Somebody beat him up real good. His lip is split in three different places, his left eye is swollen shut entirely, and his face has more purple on it than normal flesh tone.

"I don't know," he answers, his voice raw and hoarse. He has bruises around his throat, like he'd been choked as well.

"Shelby," Wyatt urges. "Just come and sit. Let him talk."

I don't want to come and sit. I want this kid to tell me where my daughter is. I want to hit him myself for luring her away from me. But for once, I take Wyatt's advice and sit across the table from the kid.

"Talk," Judge orders, dropping down at the table with us, a beer clutched in his hand.

"The last time I saw her, Hayden was okay," the kid informs us. "But my uncle saw you. He saw you questioning me, and he saw that I had Hayden's phone. I was supposed to get rid of it, along with her backpack."

"Who's your uncle?" That question comes from GP.

"Randall McDade."

All the men around the room start talking at once, angry questions coming from every corner. It scares me, so it's not a shock when the kid shrinks back in his chair.

On instinct, I reach out and place my hand on his. "Please," I whisper. "Hayden is my daughter. I know you're scared, but focus on me now, okay?"

He nods.

"Where is Hayden?"

"I don't know. Once my uncle saw me with you," he says, looking to Wyatt, "he was really angry. He took me out back and punished me."

"By punishing you, do you mean he beat the shit out of you?" Judge asks, his nostrils flaring in anger.

He nods. "He knew I'd kept that phone, and said I was a traitor. He said…" A sob rips from his throat, and like a tidal wave of emotion, he breaks down. "Please," he cries. "He has my sister. He said the only way he will keep the men away is if I bring him more girls. I never meant to hurt Hayden. I just wanted to keep my sister safe."

I frown at Wyatt, confused.

Luckily, Judge seems to get it. "So you're saying your uncle has your sister? That he promised to keep her out of danger as long as you keep bringing him girls?"

The kid nods.

"And when he saw you with the phone and Hash over there, he figured you for a traitor?"

The kid nods again. "He punished me. I was unconscious in the alley behind the store until the nighttime. And when I went home, my house was on fire."

"Do you think your uncle set that fire?" Judge asks.

"Yes. He must have moved the girls. I don't know where they are, and my sister…"

"Okay," Judge says, trying to soothe the crying boy. "Your name's Kevin, right?"

He nods.

"Kevin. Go back, and tell me the story from the beginning."

For the next twenty minutes, we all sit silent, listening as Kevin reveals a story that no child should ever have to tell. His mother had passed away four years ago, and his father had walked out when his sister was born. That meant their only living relative was their uncle, Randall.

His sister was only eight years old then, and Kevin himself had been twelve. Randall hadn't even given them time to grieve. He'd already had two young girls in his basement, and each night at eight o'clock, men would come and pay him to spend time with those girls.

He was going to put Kevin's sister, Natalie, in the basement with them. He was going to sell her.

"I begged him not to do it," Kevin asserts. "I told him I'd do anything, and that's when we made the deal. I could come and go as I pleased, and he would keep Natalie away from those men as long as I brought him another girl every few months. I thought I could find a way to escape, but he's always watching. He keeps Natalie close, and he lets those men see her, but never touch her."

This time, he looks at me, his one good eye as red as blood. "I'm sorry about your daughter. I never wanted any of this, but I didn't know what else to do. And now they're gone, and I don't know where any of them are, and I ..." Sobs cut off his words. As both a mother, and as a human being, I can't let this go on.

I stand from my chair and approach him, wrapping my arms around him. "Shh," I soothe, pressing him tight to my chest. "You're safe now, and these are the good guys. They're going to help you save your sister and Hayden."

The only sound in the room is my soft whispers of encouragement, and the sobs of a broken boy. The men allow us that time, each of them likely itching to get their hands on that bastard Randall. I know that's what I'm feeling, even though I'm trying to keep it together.

Finally, Kevin sniffs and pulls away, offering me a weak smile, pulling at the cuts on his lips. "Thank you."

I smile back, giving him one last squeeze of reassurance before I let him go.

Wiping his eyes, he sits up straight and meets Wyatt's gaze. "I saw the patch on your jacket and knew you could help me. My uncle was there, though. He was right behind us, listening to everything."

"The other man in the shop," Wyatt mutters.

"You've got to help them," Kevin pleads. "Uncle Randall's losing it, and now that he's burned down his own house, I don't know what he'll do. I'm afraid he's going to do something worse to the girls."

Judge clamps his hand down on Kevin's shoulder. "Don't you worry, bud. We're gonna end that motherfucker."

Hashtag

"HOW DO you want to play this, Judge?"

He leans back against his chair and nods toward me. "Hash is lead on this. His kid, his game plan."

Twat Knot and Stone Face shoot him a look, and it takes me aback. Judge has never handed over control to someone like this. It's an honor, and terrifying, all at the same time, the burden being squarely on my shoulders to guarantee Hayden and my brothers return home.

"Well?" Karma asks. "How we doing this?"

"We follow the kid. He's our ace in the hole."

"You mean that kid who lured your daughter out for his uncle's trafficking ring? Yeah, that sounds solid," GP sneers.

"I'm with him," Karma interjects. "You can't trust

him. This could all be a sick and twisted fucking game of cat and mouse."

"I never said I trust him, but he came to me for help. He's desperate, and I think we can use that to our advantage. He has no place to go. If we can get him on board, we'll get him to reach out to his uncle. He gets us his location, we get Hayden."

"What happens if the uncle ghosts us? You got nothing but a kid who knows where our clubhouse is located. He puts us all at risk. You need to get rid of him."

I shoot a hard glare at Stone. His negative Nancy bullshit from the moment Shelby came back is wearing thin. I don't know what it is about my situation that's bringing out the asshole in him, but I'm about two seconds away from punching his fucking lights out.

"Fuck you, man. That kid is no more a threat to us than he is to anyone else."

Stone's body tenses the second my mouth closes. Yeah, big man. Get pissed. It'll make the fight more fun. It's been a long time coming.

"The kid is our trump card, asshole. He knows how his uncle works, and how to get in touch with him. All we need is a location, and only he can get that for us."

Stone Face glares at me. The air in the room around us is so brittle, I think if I reach out and swipe at him, he'll snap into pieces. And if he doesn't, then I'll kick his ass. I start to shove away from the table, but Judge looks over at me. It doesn't take a mind reader to see what his face is trying to convey to me in silence. *Check the emotional bullshit and lead.*

"Look, I know this is my problem, but this kid is our only way. Without him, Hayden will likely be moved across the border in a matter of days, if she isn't on her way there already. I made Shelby a promise to bring her home, and I'm going to fucking do it, even if I have to do it on my own."

Each man sitting around the table looks to each other before returning their stares to me.

"How will you get him in contact with the uncle?"

"He has a couple of numbers for him. He calls, gets the uncle to agree to take him back into the fold, and then we follow."

"What's to say he'll take the kid back?"

"The kid is his bait for the girls, the linchpin of his entire business. No kid, no girls. With the kid's sister still in play, he'll think he's coming back for her. It'll work."

Stone starts to argue yet again, but I stop him short. "He'll call on a burner phone. He makes the call in front of all of us, on speaker."

"Do it," Judge commands without any further argument. I push away from the table and stalk out the door to find Kevin sitting near Shelby on one of the leather couches in the center of the common room. His eyes grow wide when he spots me, and moves closer to Shelby.

"Come with me, big man. You've got a call to make."

Kevin trembles as he stands up. I feel for him, I do. He's lived a shit life, and has been put through the ringer —if his story checks out—but he's the reason his uncle has my daughter. Had he not brought her into his mess, she'd be safe with her mom back in Beckettville, and I'd still be in the dark. It's a double-edged sword of fucked-up.

Kevin walks ahead of me into the room, and I motion for him to sit down in an open chair. Burnt closes the door behind us. Retrieving the burner phone from my pocket, I hand it to him. His face pales.

"Call him, on speaker. Tell him you want to come back."

He quivers, nervously looking to the men sitting around him. "But I don't."

"You want to help Hayden, right?" The kid nods his head slowly. "We have to find out where they are. You convince him, get us a location, and we'll do the rest."

His hand shakes when he takes the phone away from me. Looking up at me one more time, he begins to dial. The phone starts to ring and I reach down, pressing the speakerphone button. It rings six times before someone finally picks up.

"What?" the gruff voice answers.

"Uncle Randall?" his voice wavers. "It's me, Kevin."

"The fuck do you want, you little shit?"

"I want to come home." He begins to cry, adding to the effect of our plot. The uncle doesn't know that his tears aren't for him, but for the forcible lies spewing from his mouth.

"Why the hell would I want to take you back, boy? Your little stunt nearly cost me everything, after all the shit I've done for you and your ungrateful sister. When you had no place to go, I took you in."

"I know, and I'm sorry," he cries harder. "I really screwed up. I won't do it again. I'll do whatever you want me to do. Please, let me come home."

The other end of the line grows quiet. Was Kevin convincing enough to make this work? Everything depends on his uncle believing his story. He just needs to take the damn bait.

"I'll tell you what, Kevin. I'm feeling a little generous today. I'll make you a deal."

"O–Okay…" he stammers. "What do I have to do?"

"Bring me another girl. Your little gamer girl is going to fetch me a pretty penny when I sell her, but I'm going to need another one to replace her. You get me a girl, you can come home."

My jaw clenches at his mention of Hayden. He's going to pay for even thinking about her when I get my hands on him. The beating he gave his nephew will pale in comparison for what I have in mind for him.

Kevin's face drains of all color. "Do it," I mouth at him.

"I'll do it," he relents, his head hanging low.

"That's my boy. I'll pick you both up tomorrow evening at the park. Six o'clock. Don't be late. Oh, and Kevin? You don't show up with the girl, you might as well not show up at all, because what I did to you last time is nothing compared to what I'll do to Natalie."

His uncle hangs up, leaving Kevin staring at the phone.

"I can't do what he wants."

I place my hand on his shoulder and grip it tightly. "Leave it to us. Why don't you go on back out there with Shelby." He does as he's asked with no protest. When the door closes behind him, the room erupts.

"You aren't seriously considering grabbing some girl and handing her over, Judge," Twat Knot argues.

"How the fuck are we going to get a girl to agree to be bait?" Karma adds. "No hang-around is going to willingly get kidnapped for us. They're here for fun, not shit like this."

"I think I have a suggestion!" Judge yells out over the noise.

"Floor is yours, Prez."

He shoves up from his seat and stands at the head of the table.

"We ask Lindsey to be the bait."

"You've got to be out of your mind, old man. She hasn't been out of the hospital for more than a couple of weeks, and you want her to voluntarily be kidnapped? No fucking way!" Karma roars from his seat. "Over my dead body will she be bait."

If you didn't know the guy or his wandering cock, you'd think he had feelings for her, but he hasn't paid a lick of attention to her since she came back. In fact, he's given her a wide berth the few times she's been around. His reaction is a bit of a shock.

"I don't like it any more than you do, but she's the best option we have. My niece will pique this Randall's interest. She looks younger than she is, and has a good head on her shoulders. With her psychology background, she can use it to her advantage."

"I think Judge has a point. Hashtag could put a tracker on her. If things go south, she can talk her way out."

Karma turns on him. "You think so, GP? How about you send in Blair? She fits the bill too."

"Fuck you, man."

"It's an honest question. If Lindsey fits, so does Red. It's only fair we put both of their names into the hat."

GP comes flying out of his chair, stopping shy of slamming into Karma. Judge swiftly shifts, shoving his large frame between the two raging beasts and the lit powder keg.

"Enough!" Judge shouts. "The two of you need to park your asses, now. Move!"

Both GP and Karma do as they're ordered, begrudgingly.

"I know this club asks a lot of the women around us, but Lindsey is my blood. I'd never suggest her for this if I thought she'd be in danger."

Karma snarls out loud at Judge's decision and storms out of the room.

"What are we going to do about him?" I ask Judge.

"Leave him be. He'll come around. You go get shit rolling with the tracker, and I'll call Lindsey."

Chapter 23

Shelby

"I DON'T EXACTLY LOOK like a twelve-year-old," Lindsey huffs, looking at herself in the mirror.

"You look great," I assure her. "You look young, and I'm pretty sure that's all this asshole cares about."

Lindsey wrinkles her nose in disgust, pulling the brush through her hair a few more times. I come up behind her and place a hand on her arm. "Thank you for doing this. Truly."

She meets my gaze in the mirror. "This is going to work, Shelby. Guys like this make mistakes, and I know exactly what to watch for. We're going to get your girl back."

"Knock-knock," Judge calls from the other side of the door. "Let's roll, ladies."

A knot forms in my belly as I watch Lindsey take a

deep breath. If she feels any fear at all about what she's about to do, she doesn't show it on the outside. She walks out that door with her head held high.

Two identical dark blue vans sit outside the clubhouse with their sliding doors propped open. Every member of the club has shown up for this. Wyatt had said the Black Hoods were his family, and for the first time, I see it. They're here for Wyatt. They're here to save our daughter, and they don't even know her.

"All right," Wyatt calls out, walking into an open space in the center of the group. "This is how tonight's gonna play out. We're gonna drop Kevin and Lindsey off at the park where his uncle said to meet him. We're gonna stay in our vehicles and be discreet."

Karma shuffles from foot to foot, his jaw ticking like crazy as Wyatt talks, looking as antsy as I feel.

"When the uncle shows, we follow them home. Kevin will go inside, and if the girls are there, he's gonna hang a shirt or towel, or something, out the bedroom or bathroom window. That'll be our signal. Until we get that signal, we don't step in."

"What if that bastard does something to Lindsey?" Karma snarls.

"He won't have time," Wyatt replies. "We aren't going to be waiting around for hours. And Lindsey's smart. She can talk to him."

Karma curses and walks to the back of the group. Wyatt answers a couple more questions, and then they're all piling into the vans. Just before they slide the door shut on the closest one, I jump inside.

"I don't fucking think so," Wyatt snaps, reaching over my shoulder to open the door.

Fucking men. "If you think I'm sitting here while all of you go off trying to save my daughter, you're delusional. I'm coming."

"It's not safe," he insists.

"I'm coming."

Our noses are practically touching as we glare at each other, neither of us willing to budge. Finally, Judge has to step in.

"Move aside, Hash. Let the lady come along."

Wyatt shakes his head, but finally moves, allowing me to crawl the rest of the way into the open van.

It's an odd experience driving to the park. There are no seats in the van, and there are six of us back here, but none of us say a word, the air heavy with anticipation. My feelings are confusing. I'm worried about Lindsey, and about what could go wrong. I'm excited at the chance to get Hayden back tonight, and can only pray that she's still untouched.

"Okay, kid." Wyatt pulls into a space amongst the trees. Handing Kevin a burner phone, he taps it. "My number is one on speed dial. It's the only one you should be calling."

Kevin tucks it into his pocket, sounding terrified when he asks, "What do I say to him?"

Judge leans over and grasps his face in his hands, looking him straight in the eyes. "You tell him you didn't say shit about him. You don't tell him about the club. You present Lindsey like a fucking prized pig, and you signal us as fast as you fucking can so we can get all your asses out of there. You got that?"

Kevin gulps before jumping out of the van, with Lindsey following behind him.

Together, they walk through the park and over to the bench to the left. I can barely see them from back here, but GP's in the front, and he can see everything.

"They're sitting on the bench," he says, peering through a pair of binoculars. "They're chatting. They look like a pair of teenagers off on a date."

Karma shifts next to me, but he doesn't speak.

GP leans forward in his seat. "And there he is. He's talking to the kid. The kid just handed over the phone we gave him. Uncle Pedophile threw it on the ground, and now he's stomping on it."

The play-by-play GreenPeace is giving sounds totally ridiculous, but I listen intently nonetheless.

"Now they're walking."

I think of poor Kevin and the ocean of tears he'd cried last night, and my heart hurts for him. He had come to us for help, and we'd sent him right back into the lion's den.

"He just shoved Lindsey into his van. I can't tell from here, but I think he hit her, maybe knocked her out. She's not moving."

A few more minutes pass, and then GP throws the van in drive, turning around to follow Kevin and his uncle's van. They pass just as we come to the stop sign in front of us. As they go by, Kevin's bruised and swollen face peers back at us from the passenger's side window, looking absolutely terrified.

Me too, buddy. Me too.

Hashtag

WE DRIVE for nearly three hours until the van takes an exit off of I-35, just north of Laredo. The area is remote. There's nothing here—no businesses, no homes. Not even a fucking tumbleweed. It's the perfect place to hide, and the worst place possible for us not to be spotted. I hadn't planned for that.

"Isn't there a border crossing in Laredo?" Shelby questions.

"There's one going into Juárez, but we're a good twenty miles from that." Too close for comfort as far as I'm concerned.

"You don't think he's planning to take them across the border, do you?"

"I think that's exactly where he's taking them, but he won't get that far, Shel." I keep my voice as even as possible, but there's a part of me that's just as skeptical as she is. If we fail, the chances of getting Hayden back are slim to none. She'll be moved around until there's no trace of her left for us to find. We can't let that happen.

Her eyes stay on the road ahead of us, but I can feel the tension like a storm surge on the banks of the ocean.

"Ease up on the distance," I say, realizing just how close we're getting. GP slows down, adding several car lengths between our van and Kevin's uncle's. Grabbing the radio off the dash, I call back to the rest of the club following behind us.

"Pull off somewhere," I order. "It's so open out here, he'll spot us a mile away. We'll keep on him and radio back when he stops."

"Ten-four," Priest responds. "We passed a hotel a few miles back. I'll swing in there and await your call. Stay safe, brother."

I put the radio back into place and keep my eyes trained on the piece of shit van. Desert flatlands surround us, and even though he's not close, the plumes of dust behind him give him away.

About twenty minutes later, he suddenly turns off onto a dirt road and floors it, kicking up dust behind him.

"Do you want me to follow him?" GP asks.

I consider it. Even with the dust, he'll see us, taking away the element of surprise. I don't want any more distance between us and the van, but it's too risky. We have to hang back. I peer down to the tracker's signal on my satellite laptop. The signal is still going strong.

"He's slowing down. Pull off over there by that line of trees. There looks to be some kind of house out there, which might be his hidey-hole."

GP maneuvers our van as I ask, and nestles us close behind the trees, obscuring us from view. Checking the mirrors, I see no one around us and exit the vehicle, leaving the door open wide. I shift the laptop to the van seat with the tracking software and a map of the area side by side on the screen.

"Hop out of there, and bring the radio and binoculars with you," I tell Shelby. "You stay in the van, GP, in case we need to make a clean getaway."

I push through some of the thicker parts of the brush until I find a good spot. Shelby slips in behind me and shoves the binoculars over my shoulder. Bringing them up to my eyes, I look for the van through the thick dust. It takes a few minutes before I can spot it. The van comes to a stop near the house I'd seen from the road, and Randall comes around to the side door.

Kevin jumps from the passenger seat and stands next to him. The side door of the van opens, and he reaches inside. I don't recognize the first girl he pulls out, but her body is nearly limp as she falls against him. Kevin helps the girl inside the house while Randall waits outside. Reaching in a second time, he drags Lindsey out, and just like the first girl, she's unsteady on her feet. He's drugged them.

"Give me the radio." She hands it to me, and I press it up close to my mouth.

"Got eyes on Lindsey. She's okay, but she's clearly out of it."

Karma mutters a string of curses in the background.

"Calm your ass down, K, I'm trying to hear," Judge growls. "Any sign of Hayden?"

"Not yet, but he just took Lindsey inside. He's got a little house out here in the boonies."

Kevin comes back out, and Hayden steps out of the van. She's steadier on her feet, but she looks exhausted, covered in dirt from head to toe.

"She's there," I relay back to Judge. Shelby shoves me over and snatches the binoculars from me. "She was the last girl out of the van. He's got another girl with them."

"Oh, my baby," Shelby cries when she sees her. "That's the same outfit she had on the day she disappeared. She looks like she's lost weight."

Grabbing the binoculars back, I take another look. It's hard to make out from this distance, but she looks unharmed outside of the filth. I watch until she disappears from view, and the door slams shut behind her. Stepping out from the trees, I hand the binoculars to Shelby and head back to the van to watch the tracker. The beacon flashes. He hasn't found it yet.

"What's going on?" Karma demands over the radio.

"Everyone's inside the house. Tracker is still active."

"So we go in. It's one guy against ten of us. There's no need to wait."

"No," I snap. "Kevin will signal us when the time is right. If we bum-rush our way in there, he'll kill the girls before we can even get close."

Karma growls into the radio, "I don't fucking like this, man. We're putting too much faith in this kid."

"I've got eyes on the place. He makes a move, I'll see him. I'm sending Priest our location now. The sun's going down fast, so it'll be dark by the time you get here." Pulling my phone from my pocket, I fire off the text with our coordinates.

"How the fuck are you going to see in the dark? He could move them and you'd never know," Karma argues back.

"Night vision, dumbass. I had Priest pick up some new toys for us. They're in the van."

Silence comes from the other end.

"We're on our way."

Laying the radio on the ground next to my laptop, I

turn to Shelby, who still stands in the brush with her gaze locked on the house that holds our daughter. She leans against me when I move behind her.

"She's alive," she whispers. "I thought..." A sob snatches her breath away.

"Shh, Shel. I told you I'd find her. Just a little longer until she's back and safe with us."

"What if they've done something to her?"

"Then we deal with it as a family." I wrap my arms around her neck, holding her tight. We stand like that, watching together, for thirty minutes before the rumble of another vehicle pulls up behind our van.

"Stay here, and keep watch," I whisper to her. With my hand on the gun, I step out of the tree line and sigh in relief. The cavalry is here.

Karma charges headlong into the trees with Shelby, leaving the rest of us outside.

"Any movement?" Priest asks as he exits the van, dressed all in black.

"None. It's been quiet."

"Quiet is good." Reaching back into the van, he tosses me a bag. I unzip it, and find my own set of dark clothing. Pulling out the long-sleeved T-shirt, I take the one I have on off and slip it over my head.

"You weren't kidding about being out in the open

here," Burnt remarks when he joins us. "The only thing we have going for us is the darkness."

"There's been no traffic since we've been out here. It's just us and them. The odds are in our favor."

"Let's keep it that way."

Karma stomps out of the tree line and beelines for the back of the van.

"He still pissed?"

"Pissed ain't the word I would use to describe his mood," Twat Knot declares. "He bitched the entire drive down here. Thank fuck for headphones, man, or I'd have thrown his ass out on the interstate."

A laugh escapes my lips, but lasts only seconds when my laptop begins to beep, and I feel as if the ground has been yanked out from under me.

"The fuck is that?" Karma questions.

"The tracker's offline!" I yell, rushing toward my laptop. A red bar flashes above the screen. Disconnected. He's found it. The fucker found it on Lindsey. Fuck, fuck, fuck!

"He's outside," Shelby calls out to us. I burst into a run and fly into the brush, snatching the binoculars from her.

The uncle is outside the house, gun in hand. He knows we're here. There's no time to waste now. We have to move in.

Shelby

"WHAT DO WE DO, PREZ?" Karma asks, his gun at the ready.

"Let me fucking think!" Judge snaps, running forward and snatching the binoculars from Hashtag's hands. "Fuck!"

He watches for a few more moments, his jaw clenched tight. "Okay, he's gone back inside. Shelby, you get your ass back in the van. The rest of you, we're going to move in. We don't know for sure if that motherfucker is onto us or not. He could just be paranoid."

"There are no windows on the south side of the house, which means we go in low and fast. We reach the building and we head in, SWAT style—everyone armed, everyone alert. You got it?"

The men around me all nod, or call out their affirmations, ready to go. "Get your guns, boys," Judge orders. "It's time to take out a fucking pervert."

Watching them all strap on holsters and bulletproof vests is surreal. It's like watching a Hollywood movie, but this time, there's no guarantee that the good guys will win in the end.

"Get in the van, baby." Wyatt, approaching from the side, pulls me into his chest. "We've got this."

I look up at him with tears burning in my eyes. "Be careful, handsome."

He grins. It's what I used to call him when we were young. "Ah, you do love me," he teases, placing a kiss on the tip of my nose. "I'm getting our girl back. This family is long overdue for a fucking reunion."

I watch, my entire body trembling as the group splits up, all of them crouched low to the ground, guns clutched in their hands.

God, if you're listening, I know you and me aren't real good friends, but I need a favor. I don't have much family, and what I do have is in danger right now. Please, can you take care of them?

I stand frozen until I can't see them anymore. I try using the binoculars, but the area they're in is dark, and they're staying low. They're going to make this work.

A crash rips through the quiet, and I swing the binoculars around to see Kevin's uncle barging out the door.

My heart drops to my feet. There are two young girls in front of him, along with Kevin.

But it's the girl he has clutched to his chest, a gun jammed into her temple, that causes my knees to go weak. Hayden.

I gaze in horror as he barks something at the three children out front. They're too far away for me to see their expressions, but from the way they're moving, I can tell they're afraid.

Desperate, I look in the direction the Black Hoods had gone, and see a flash of something midway between the van and the house, and then the outline of a few of them. They've stayed together. *They're not close enough.*

The children climb into the man's rusted-out van, as he follows behind them with Hayden. When he gets to it, he grabs her by the hair and shoves her inside, causing her to cry out in pain, the sound echoing through the night. And that's when I make my decision. It's going to be me who kills Randall. I don't give a fuck what Judge wants, or what Wyatt says. His blood will be on my hands, and I'm so full of rage right now, I'll gladly bathe myself in it.

He rounds the vehicle at lightning speed, and before I can blink, the van's speeding down the long dirt road.

I look back to Wyatt and the others who are still so far

away. *He's going to get away. He's going to make it across the border, and then we'll never find her.*

Without another thought, I run back to the van and jump inside, sliding the side door closed behind me. The key is in the ignition when I jump into the driver's seat, and I bring the engine to life. I don't allow the doubts I feel to gather in my head. I can't wait for Wyatt and the guys. There's no time.

I don't try to go incognito, seeing as Randall already knows we're here.

Even at top speed, it feels like I'm not gaining enough ground. The area around us is open and flat, and so fucking dark. I press the pedal to the floor, willing this jalopy to morph into the Batmobile, or an Indy 500 race car, but it doesn't happen. My speed is already maxed out.

Approaching the interstate, Randall turns onto it. He's heading right by me, but on a different road. *Fuck that, asshole.*

Making a decision that could either save my daughter or end all our lives, I yank the wheel to the right, and without dropping speed, I zoom across the plain between the two roads. The chances of making it across this land-scape without hitting a pothole, or obliterating the front end of this vehicle on a rock are slim, but I chance it anyway, knowing that God and I now have an understanding. He's going to make sure I get my kiddo back. A roar rips from my throat as I move, rivaling the scream of any fun-seeker riding their favorite roller coaster. Except mine is a scream of fear, not thrill.

Finally, I'm on the interstate and spin the wheel, righting the vehicle in the direction of the Mexican border, and now just a few feet behind them. "Come on, asshole," I mutter, speeding up and getting even closer.

At this time of night, there's not another soul on the road. My heart gallops in my chest when I see a sign appear that makes it stutter before going even faster: Mexico - 2 miles.

He's going to make it. He's going to find a place to cross illegally, and I'm going to lose Hayden forever.

A hole appears in the windshield just above my head, and I stare at it in shock, realizing that Randall's shooting at me through his window. Another hole appears right beside it, and I scream, ducking low.

A road appears on the left, and Randall cranks the wheel, his van going off the ground on one side before righting itself.

Fuck, fuck, fuck! What am I going to do?

A corner appears up ahead, and when Randall slows to take it, I decide my next move. I don't slow. I press the pedal down harder, praying to God that he takes care of the children.

Hitting it is like a dream. It all happens both in slow motion and hyperspeed. I don't have time to react, but I feel every vibration and hear every sound. The front bumper of my van collides with the ass end of Randall's, and then I'm spinning.

I scream as the walls around me cave in as I roll, losing track of where Randall and the kids should be. By the time I come to a stop, my head is pounding, the glass around me is shattered, and my vision is blurred.

"Hayden," I croak. "Hayden."

My last thought before the darkness takes over is: I think I just killed my own daughter.

Hashtag

"COME ON, man, hit the fucking gas. Shelby's out there on her own!" I scream at GP from the passenger seat.

"I've got it down to the floor. I can't make this thing go any faster." I know he's trying to catch up with them, but every second counts right now. I don't care if we end up in a high-speed chase with the police tailing us. I have to get to Shelby and Hayden before it's too late.

"See anything?" Judge asks from the back.

"Nothing."

"She's out there, son. Both of them are."

"You mean the three of them are. Lindsey put her ass on the line for the two of you, and she's stuck now," Karma interjects. I turn and look at him, finding his large frame plastered against one side of the van, his eyes dark.

Empty almost, just like mine. He's got more skin in this game than he wants to admit.

"I'm very aware of the situation my niece is in. That shit isn't lost on me."

"If I—I mean, *we*, lose her to this bullshit..." Shaking his head, he looks away.

"We won't," Judge assures him.

"We'll see about that."

My leg bounces like a fucking druggy itching for his next fix, while GP drives in the direction that she and Randall went. What the fuck was she thinking? We could've made it back to the van in time, but she took off like a bat out of hell without us.

We're only miles now from the border. If they make it that far, I'll lose Hayden, probably Shelby too. I can't have that.

"You see that? Look there." Judge points between the front seats toward a plume of smoke visible in the sky a few miles ahead of us.

"Right there!" I bellow. "GP, follow that smoke!"

He makes a quick right turn onto a side road before veering the van off-road. We bounce hard across the dusty earth underneath us.

My mind goes into overdrive, assessing what we could find under the smoke.

Are we too late? Is Hayden gone and Shelby collat-

eral damage? My hands grip the dashboard as I do the only thing I can. I pray to a God who's never given me any hope before to not take them away from me. Not before I have the chance to tell them both how much I love them.

The van coasts in the air when GP hits a hill too fast, but he keeps it under control. The van, and everyone else inside of it, lands with a thud when we make contact with the ground again.

"Fuck, man," someone groans from the back. "I think you gave me a concussion."

"Ain't my fault you don't wear your seatbelt."

"There aren't any seatbelts back here, asshole."

Twat Knot's head pops up from between the two seats with his finger extended. "Look."

In the distance, two large objects come into view, smoke pouring out of them both. My eyes don't move. The two objects turn into two different vans lying on their sides. Fuck. We found them.

GP comes to a skidding stop, and I'm out of the van before anyone else. My feet pound the pavement beneath me when I come up on the first van. I jump up on the passenger side and rip open the door. There, in the driver's seat, sits Shelby. She's alive.

"Are you hurt?"

"I'm trapped." Her voice is calm, but hoarse. "I tried to stop him, but wrecked us instead."

"I'm going to get you out of here, baby." I turn back to look at my brothers rushing up behind me. "Stone! GP! Give me a hand. We gotta flip this van. Shelby's trapped."

"No," Shelby croaks. "Hayden first. Go check on Hayden."

"Not until I get you out, baby. I'm not leaving you," I argue back.

Stone shoves in next to me and takes in the scene. "We're going to need a winch to get this pulled over. I think we can rig something up."

"Do it!" I holler.

"We're going to get you out. Hang in there, Shel."

"You need to go check on Hayden, please!"

My mind and my heart go to war with each other. I want to be here with Shelby, but I need to be with Hayden too. I glance over at the other van. No one's stirring inside or outside of it. Karma's screaming and yanking at the van door as smoke begins to pour more heavily out of it.

"Go," GP mutters, shoving me aside, while Stone drags a chain from our van. "We got your girl. Go get your daughter and Lindsey."

"Go, Wyatt," she pleads. "She needs you."

I look at her one more time before leaping from the side of the toppled van and toward the other one. Karma pulls hard on the door, but it doesn't budge. I grab hold of it, and together, we pull and yank, and finally force it open partway, smoke pouring out from the opening. Karma squeezes his large body into the space and disappears from view. Within seconds, a girl is shoved toward me from inside. I catch her, dragging her out onto the ground, but it's not Hayden or Lindsey.

Come on, Hayden. Please be okay.

A second form pushes out of the van. This time it's Lindsey, coughing and choking on the smoke as she comes through. Reaching out for her, I help steady her down to the ground and lead her over to the grassy side of the road, far away from the smoke.

"My daughter?" I ask. "Is she...?"

Lindsey coughs hard and shakes her head, but Karma's voice calls out over the commotion.

"Hash! I got her!"

I bolt back to the van just as Karma emerges through the hole. He reaches down, tugging and pulling until the last girl is hoisted out. Her head is turned away from me, but I hear her gasping for air as Karma tends to her. When she finally turns, our eyes connect, and my heart flutters back to life.

It's Hayden. My daughter is alive.

"Come on, kiddo. Let's get you down," Karma offers. She leans over the edge on her butt, sliding down into my open arms. Her eyes instantly lock onto mine as I hold her small little body in my arms. Of all the moments I've imagined holding my own child for the first time, I'd imagined them as an infant, not a teenager. But holding her now takes all those regrets and firsts I'd missed far from my mind. This moment—our first moment—is the single best moment of my life. So many things could have gone wrong today, but here she is.

"Hayden?" She's really here—my daughter. "You okay? Any broken bones? Cuts?"

"No," she gasps. "I'm okay." She stares up at my face, reaching her hand weakly to press it against my sweaty cheek. "You're my dad, aren't you?"

"I am," I tell her. "You're going to be okay now, honey. I've got you. You're safe."

"Where's Mom?"

"She's trapped in the other van, but we're getting her out. I need to put you down now, honey, but this man's going to take good care of you. I need to go help her." I gently place her next to Lindsey, with Karma buzzing around her like an old mother hen.

"Watch Hayden," I demand before returning to Shelby. A loud crash comes from behind us as her van returns to its wheels. Shelby's eyes connect with mine before looking over at the ditch, spying Hayden. A smile forms on her lips.

"Hash! Over here!" Judge yells out from the other side of Randall's van. I switch directions, and come to a skidding halt when I see the body on the ground, unmoving.

"Is it the kid?" I ask on my approach.

"No, it's the uncle. He was thrown from the van."

"He dead?"

"Yeah. Neck looks snapped. Probably died on impact."

I wish I could say that his death gave me a sense of relief, but it was too quick for someone like him. He deserved to suffer for his transgressions. For all the girls he ripped away from their families and sold into sexual slavery. His ending did not match the one I'd had planned for him, but all best-laid plans tend to go to shit anyway. He's no longer my problem, but it does leave the kid.

"You see the kid?"

"No. He wasn't with the girls?"

Shit. He's still in there. I climb back up on the side and yank open the passenger door. Inside, lying against the center console between the front seats is Kevin, motionless. Pushing myself inside, I reach out for him and grip his arm tightly. He's like lead weight as I pull, but with a few tugs, I get him free and halfway out of the van. His chest moves up and down slowly. Thank fuck, he's still alive.

Burnt appears next to me and helps get him out the rest of the way. With him on one side and me on the other, we carry him by his arms to the side of the road with Lindsey and Hayden.

Hayden cries out when she sees him. Leaning her thin frame over his, she hugs him on the ground, sobbing against his chest. "Kevin!"

The other girl comes forward, her face pale as a ghost. She stares down at him with horror and fear. I watch with pride as Hayden takes her tiny hand and pulls her down beside her. "Kevin," she sobs. "Kevin, please don't leave me."

I hate leaving them, but I have no choice. "You stay here with him. I'll be right back."

I pivot on my heels, just as the van Shelby's in catches fire. Flames and smoke shoot from beneath the hood, and my heart sinks. The gas line's been severed. We need to move, fast.

Shelby

MY GAZE MEETS Wyatt's through the shattered windshield, behind plumes of flame and smoke. *Oh, God.*

Reaching beside me for the hundredth time, I yank on the door handle, but it's not even attached to the door anymore. Even though the guys had gotten the van flipped right-side up, the roof is caved in so badly, I could never fit through the window.

Thick black smoke rolls through the opening from under the hood, and I struggle to breathe. I cover my face with my T-shirt, but it's no help.

"Hurry!" I cry out. GP, Priest, and Wyatt all yank on my door, while the others work at different ends of the van, trying anything they can to get it to open somewhere.

"We're coming, baby," Wyatt hollers.

I watch in horror as the flickering flames lick out from beneath the hood, growing higher and hotter. "We gotta hurry, boys!" someone yells.

Metal pings, and the sound is deafening as I sit helpless, waiting for a miracle. Acrid smoke invades my nostrils and mouth, winding its way into my lungs, choking the breath out of me.

"Fucking Christ!"

"It's too hot."

"Don't you fucking stop!" Wyatt screams. "None of you stop, not until she's out."

The flames are coming in through the window now, and I know it's too late. I look over to where Hayden sits, cradling Kevin in her arms.

I'm going to die, but I'm going to die knowing that my baby girl is safe. She's with her father. She loves me, Wyatt loves me, and they both know that I love them. At least, I hope…

"Wyatt!" Tears stream down my cheeks, but there are no sobs. My fate is sealed in that moment, and I'm okay with it. "I love you!"

"No!" Wyatt shouts, his face flashing with anger. He kicks at the edge of the door, and it moves just a little, but we're out of time.

"Wyatt," I try again. "I never stopped loving you."

"Stop it," he snarls at me, kicking at the widening gap in the door. "Stop fucking saying goodbye to me."

I can barely breathe now. There's more smoke than air, and my head's bobbing as I cling to consciousness. I can hear Hayden screaming from across the road, but the smoke is too thick to see her now.

"Take care of her," I whisper, but the fire is roaring louder, so I'm not sure he hears me.

"Priest! Grab that crowbar!"

The darkness closes in. "I love you."

"I smell gas!"

"I know! Move your ass!"

"Goodbye, handsome."

The world fades away, taking my weightless body into the abyss.

Hashtag

THE LAST TWENTY-FOUR hours have been a whirlwind. Everything had happened so fast. And now Hayden is here, and I can't help but find my heart torn between happiness and guilt. I'd wanted a family so bad, and here I have one. But obtaining it hadn't been easy. I might have my family, but people were hurt in the process.

"She awake yet?" Priest asks when he stops by with some food. Sitting it down on my desk, he walks over to us.

"Not yet."

Priest stares down at her sleeping form, stating matter-of-factly, "She will be. How are you holding up?"

"You running a confessional now?" Smirking at him, he scowls back. "I'm as good as I can be."

"Let me know if you need anything."

He slips out of the room, and I return to watching her sleep. My poor girl had been through so much. The second I held her small frame in my lap as we drove from the scene of the crash, she fell asleep. Even as we moved her inside of the clubhouse, she didn't stir, exhaustion setting in once she knew she was safe.

The doctor had looked her over, and I'd been relieved to know we'd gotten to her in time. Whatever that bastard had planned for Hayden, he hadn't been able to carry it out.

She was lucky, and if GP's most recent rundown of everyone's status still holds true, she's not the only one.

Lindsey is dealing with some smoke inhalation, but is otherwise in good shape. She's getting fluids to force the drugs out of her system, and Karma hasn't left her side. Kevin and the other girl, who we now know as his sister, Natalie, are being cared for by the doctor in one of the other rooms under Judge's watchful eye.

These are all reasons for celebration, but watching Hayden sleep in my bed for over twelve hours is breaking the slim hold I have on reality. The darkness swirling inside of me keeps rearing its ugly head, reminding me of what it had taken to bring her home safely.

"Dad?" her soft voice beckons.

Dad. A rush of happiness rockets through the darkest part of my heart. Hearing those three letters in that specific arrangement, and from this very special girl, melts away all the anger and guilt I've been fighting off all night.

The second I laid my eyes on her, she became my everything. Now, hearing her say it, nothing else could compare to this feeling. She's my daughter. My blood. My world. There's only one thing missing, though, and that's Shelby.

This moment should be shared between the three of us. My family together at last. Shelby deserved to be here for our true reunion. She wouldn't have wanted to miss this.

"How are you feeling?" I ask, shifting from my chair to the edge of the bed. Her messy brown hair sticks out from all different angles, and she couldn't be more beautiful.

"Sore." She tries to shift her body into a seated position, but struggles. I gently take her arm, helping her until she finally finds some comfort. Her eyes flit around the room, taking it all in. "Where am I?"

"My room at the clubhouse."

Her face scrunches up in confusion. "This is where you live?"

"I have a place of my own, but when I'm working on a project, it's just easier to do it here."

"You mean the illegal stuff."

This time, it's my turn to be a bit taken aback. I'd assumed Shelby told her nothing about me, but it seems my smart little girl knows more than she should.

My brow arches. "How do you know about my club?"

"Grandma Lorna," she admits with a flush of embarrassment on her face. "Grandpa wouldn't allow anyone to talk about you, but after he passed away, Grandma Lorna mentioned you once. She and Mom were arguing after the funeral at our house. They didn't know that I'd snuck into the kitchen to get some ice cream. She said your club's name, and I might have looked it up."

"Of course you did," I tease, smiling.

"It's true, then?"

"We protect people who can't protect themselves, like you."

"And Mom?" The mention of her mother sinks like a lead pellet in my belly. Protecting Shelby was all that I was trying to do, and in the end, I'd failed.

"Yes, like your mom."

She slumps back against the headboard in silent contemplation. Her brown eyes well up, but she swipes away the stray tear that dares to break through the dam she's actively trying to build up against it.

"Why didn't Mom tell me about you?"

"Your mom is a complicated woman, Hayden." She almost cracks a smile. Complicated didn't even begin to describe Shelby. She's been like the earth to my moon, in constant orbit around each other with a magnetic pull radiating between us.

"But you're my dad," she argues. "I needed a dad."

"She had her reasons, kiddo. But what matters is that I'm here now, and I always will be." I give her hand a slight squeeze for reassurance. "There's no going back now."

Her emotional dam breaks as she reaches out toward me, wrapping her thin arms around my neck, squeezing me tight. Her wet tears soak into my T-shirt, but I don't care. She needs me. She sobs against me for several minutes before pulling back.

"I never knew I needed a daughter until I met you. I know we've got a lot to learn about each other, but we've got plenty of time to do all that. What's important is that you're here, and you're safe."

Her head hangs low. "I was so stupid. I should've never gone to meet him," she laments. "We were friends. He was the first person I felt really understood me and my love for programming. None of my friends at school like computers the way I do, but on Blox World, I could be myself. I didn't have to hide."

A sentiment I too had felt around her age. None of my foster families saw me for my potential. I was just the son of a druggie who didn't fit into the cookie cutter mold of what a kid should be like. I was friendless, but when I was on a computer, an entire world of possibilities came to life for me. I bet Hayden felt the same way too. Yes, she'd made a huge mistake, one that nearly cost her her life, but I'm not going to keep her away from programming. It changed my life once, and it might just do the same for her. In a more stringent and controlled setting, of course.

"You didn't know what was on the other side of that screen. What happened isn't your fault, Hayden."

"I wish I'd never started playing that stupid game," she berates herself. "None of this would have happened if I hadn't bought it."

"Things like this happen more than you know. There are evil people in this world, pretending to be someone else online. No one your age could have realized what Kevin's uncle was making him do."

"I know."

"It might take a while, but when you're ready, and only if you're ready, maybe the two of us can play Blox World together."

She beams, looking back up to me. "Really?"

"I'd love to play it with you. You've got some tricks I'd like to learn."

Hayden reaches out for me again. She'd made a mistake, and I'd made dozens of them at her age. But, once this was all behind us, we could heal together in the safety of my oversight, and the trackers I'll be putting in every single electronic she owns until the day I die. Maybe even her car.

"Is Kevin okay?"

"He's a little beaten up, but he'll be okay." She sighs in relief. This kid may have started it all, but we both owe him a life debt. Without his help, none of this would've been possible.

"What will happen to him now?"

"Once he's back on his feet, we'll make sure he and his sister are well looked after. Both of them."

"Do you think I could see him?"

"Not yet. Kevin needs some time to process everything, and he needs to be there for his sister right now. But I promise you, when the time is right, you'll be able to see him again—under supervision." They both needed time to come to terms with their experiences. She may not realize it yet, but it will come. Maybe not today, or tomorrow, but it will. Tossing the two of them back into the mix together too soon could be a fuse to a match. She has to be ready to face what emotional dam it could break open. Thank God we have Red for when—and if—that happens.

She falls quiet, lost in her own mind.

"Do you think…"

"What is it, Hayden?"

"Do you think Mom saw me before, you know…?"

"She did, honey. She was so happy to see you safe."

A knock sounds at the door. I turn, and Judge's face peeks in through the crack.

"Who's that?" she questions nervously.

"That's Judge. He's the president of the club."

"He's scary." She eyes him up and down, moving closer to me. At her age, a guy as big as Judge would scare me too. I can't wait for her to meet Stone. He'll blow her mind.

I don't know if Judge heard her, or if he's just ignoring it, but he doesn't say anything other than, "I think you should both come next door."

Hayden looks to him, and then back to me in confusion. "What's next door?"

Grasping her arm, easing her to the edge of the bed, I help her onto her feet. "Hang on to me if you need it." She takes a few steps before she finds her footing. Judge opens the door for us as we approach. Leading us into the hallway and down to the room adjacent to my own, he inches open the door, and Hayden gasps.

"Mom!" Without hesitation, she slips away from me and rushes to her mother's bedside, albeit slowly. Shelby reaches out for her, embracing her daughter tightly against her chest, both of them sobbing loudly together at their reunion. "I'm so glad you're okay."

Shelby caresses her face. "You know I'd never leave you, baby."

"You'd better not," Hayden declares, snuggling into her even more.

"One of your dad's friends got me out of that van just in time. He saved my life," Shelby says softly. "I owe him everything."

Hayden finally releases her mother and notices Lorna sitting on the other side of the bed, Kasey flanking her. "Grandma? Aunt Kasey? What are you doing here?"

"Your dad called me." Hearing Lorna refer to me as Hayden's father seems almost foreign. Her husband had made no bones about where I stood in his eyes, but I knew I would need help, with Hayden and Shelby both unconscious. As much as I wanted to be with them both, I couldn't. I had to call in reinforcements, and Lorna graciously accepted when I sent the prospect to her house to get her. Kasey had been there as well, waiting on news. I wish I could say I was happy to see her here, but that would be a lie.

Hayden gingerly crawls up onto the bed with her mother and I watch, my heart swelling, as they alternate between chatting and crying.

"Thanks for saving my girls." I turn my attention to

Kasey, who stands beside me, her hand outstretched. I blink hard. *Was that gratitude coming from Kasey's mouth?*

"You mean, *my* girls," I correct her.

"Take good care of them." Smiling, she heads out of the room.

Judge smirks. "Look at you, mending bridges and shit."

"I wouldn't go that far. That woman is still a giant pain in my ass."

Judge throws his head back and laughs. Clapping his hand down on my shoulder, he nods toward the bed. "What are you doing standing here, dickhead? Go be with your family."

My family. The one thing I had been searching for my entire life.

Chapter 29

Shelby

"WE SURE ARE GOING to miss you around here," Serge says, helping me stuff the last of my tattoo supplies into the back of my car. "You're gonna kick ass in Austin, though. You're too talented for a shit hole place like this, anyway."

"So are you," I tell him, turning to make sure he's actually listening. "Buying this shop helped me out in a big way, Serge, but don't get stuck here. Use the business, hone your skill, broaden your horizons. But don't fucking stay here forever. You're too good for a small town like this."

Serge grins and slams the trunk closed. "Maybe someday, I'll be working for you again."

"You'd better," I tease, popping up on the tips of my toes to give him a hug.

"Now go." Turning me by the shoulders, he pushes me toward the driver's door of my car. "I hate goodbyes."

I chuckle as I climb inside. Giving him a final wave, I pull out onto the road, taking one last look at my former tattoo shop in the rearview mirror, and smile. I'd loved working for myself. I was the only tattoo shop in town, and I'd been lucky to have people here who allowed me to hone my skills.

Moving to Austin, and working at a high-end shop there, will be so much better. Less responsibility, more money, and I get to live in the house Wyatt and I had bought just two weeks ago.

After we rescued Hayden, it took some time for him to let either one of us out of his sight. I understood, so I never mentioned it. Hayden loved her father instantly. I've never seen two people connect on such a deep level as my man and our daughter.

It hadn't taken much convincing for me, or Hayden, to sell our home in Beckettville and move to Austin to live with Wyatt. We'd spent enough time apart. None of us wanted to miss any more time.

My phone rings just as I get to the outskirts of town. It's Hayden.

"Hi, honey."

"Mom, I'm going to Kevin's house to watch a movie. Dad's taking me, but I wanted to let you know too."

That's my good girl. She has taken on such shame for her own kidnapping, and the things she did to make herself more accessible to her abductors. Now she tells me where she is and who she's with at all times. And lately, that *who* she's with always seems to be Kevin.

They've connected somehow. I can't tell quite yet if it's a crush or a connection through shared trauma, but they lean heavily on each other, and Kevin's a good kid. Despite the way they'd met and what had happened, I trust him.

"Okay, kiddo. Have fun."

"I will."

"And be safe!" I shout.

"Yes, Mom."

I chuckle to myself as she disconnects. I drive the remainder of the way to my hometown, lost in my own thoughts. I pull into the clubhouse and head inside, in search of Wyatt.

"Hey, Shelby," Judge calls from the table at the back of the room.

My eyes widen. "Hey. I thought you were at home."

He frowns. "No, I'm right here. Why would you think that?"

"Because my daughter and your…" I pause, unsure of what to call him.

"Kevin?" he offers with a knowing smirk.

"Yes! Your Kevin and Hayden are supposed to be at your house watching a movie, but if you're here, that means they're there without any supervision."

Judge throws his head back and laughs, his hard belly rising and falling at my expense. "Oh, honey," he hoots. "Little Natalie is there too. They're being supervised extra hard today."

I grin back and roll my eyes. Judge had taken in Kevin and Natalie that same night. He shocked everyone, including me, on how parental he can be. He's proving himself to be one hell of a dad.

"Hey, baby," Wyatt says, coming at me from behind and swooping me up into his arms.

I smile and rest my head back on his shoulder. "Did you get the last of your stuff?"

I nod. "Yep. I have all my tattoo equipment in the car."

"Oooh," GP drawls, strolling into the room. "You gonna put some ink on your man's virgin skin?"

Wyatt glowers at him while I laugh. "He couldn't handle it," I tease, patting Wyatt on the ass.

"Fuck both of you." He narrows his eyes at GP. "Go get your shit, Shel. You get one tat. Make it a good one."

"Yeah, right," I scoff, landing a gentle slap on his chest.

"No," he says, his face serious. "Come on. I'll help you bring it in."

"Wyatt—"

"Hurry up, woman, before I change my mind."

Not about to argue with that, I hurry along behind him, following him to my car and watching as he opens the trunk. GP grabs a case, Wyatt grabs a case, and Judge comes out of nowhere and grabs my tools.

"What?" he asks when we all stare at him. "I want to watch."

It takes me about forty-five minutes to set up. I sanitize everything and scrub down an area in the center of the clubhouse common room. While I work, more of the guys show up, making me feel like I'm in some sort of a fishbowl being watched from leather wearing men on all sides.

"Whatcha gonna get, asshole?" Twat Knot chuckles. "A butterfly on your ankle?"

"No, a flower on his foot," someone else calls out.

I ignore them all, and motion for Wyatt to take a seat. "Okay, handsome. What are we doing?"

Wyatt whips his shirt over his head and tosses it onto the table. "I told you, you get one tat. Your choice of what and where. Make it count."

Suddenly, I don't feel so confident. I'm an artist, and

a fucking good one at that. But right now, I have an audience, and all of them are rooting for me to tat something stupid on the man I love. The man I love has never wanted a tattoo on his skin before, and now, he's letting me put my mark on him.

"She won't do it," Karma scoffs.

I chew on my lip, thinking about our story. About our daughter. About the struggles we've survived and the ones we still have yet to face. And then, I get an idea.

I pull on my gloves and get the ink ready. Slowly, I approach Wyatt and stand directly in front of him. Our eyes meet as I lower myself and place one leg on the right side of him, the other on the left.

"Jesus," somebody mutters, but I tune them out.

My eyes are locked on Wyatt's as I sit on his lap, his hands cupping my ass, holding me steady. "You ready?"

His nostrils flare, and butterflies erupt in my belly. *Focus, Shelby.*

I can feel his cock growing hard beneath me, and it takes a great amount of restraint not to roll my hips and grind myself against him. The audience around us forces me to pay attention to the task at hand.

I grab up the paper towel from the table and place the tattoo gun to Wyatt's muscular chest. I work quickly and efficiently, dipping the gun with ink and swiping away the excess. Wyatt's eyes never leave my face, and I've never felt more beautiful, or more desirable, than I do right now.

I switch colors three times, and when I'm finished, I use a cool cloth to wipe his skin. Finally, I grin and press my lips to his. "You're finished."

"Not quite." Placing his hands on my thighs, he grinds his cock against me.

I laugh, handing him the small mirror. "I meant your tattoo."

He grabs it out of my hand and I stand up, taking a few steps back to admire my work. Wyatt stares at the design, frozen.

"Do you like it?"

He finally looks up at me, his eyes filled with so much love. "You're amazing."

I grin, proud of the work I'd done. It's a small tattoo, but I'd put a lot of detail and precision into making it just right.

There, over his very real, beating heart, is a red, tattered, perfectly drawn heart, filled with rips and jagged lines. Along every one of those lines is a thread—a stitch. And above that is the needle with a piece of thread that curls along, forming the words, *End Game*.

He stands and pulls me into a hug. "I love you, baby," he whispers in my ear. "You are my fucking end game."

"And I wouldn't have it any other way."

Our hug lasts a long time, and I don't ever want it to end. But as it always happens in this clubhouse, the moment is disrupted when Twat Knot flops down into the chair Wyatt had just vacated and says, "My turn!"

Hashtag

"WHY DO we have to go to this party again?" Hayden grumbles from the back seat of our new Ford Explorer. I'd wanted to add a side car to one of my bikes for family trips, but Shelby had vetoed that idea, and away we came with this beast of a car. Little did she know, Hayden and I had made a trip of our own to the Harley dealership beforehand. The sidecar was already being installed on my spare bike. Better to ask for forgiveness later than permission now, right?

"A patch party is an important night for a prospect, Hay," I explain.

"Not really a place for a child, though," Shelby argues.

"We'll be long gone before the debauchery starts,

Shel. As a member, I have to be there, and it'll be nice for the two of you to meet everyone officially."

"Is Walter going to be there?" Hayden inquires.

"I don't know what you see in that beast of dog."

"He likes me."

"You mean, he likes those treats you keep taking him when you go see Blair," Shelby corrects her. "No dog can resist a cheeseburger."

Red and Hayden have really struck up a friendship after I'd asked her to come over to see Hayden. She'd been having frequent nightmares since her kidnapping. Red wouldn't tell me what the two of them had talked about, but Hayden seemed happier when they did.

The clubhouse comes into view, and every single space is taken in the front parking lot. I peer over at Shelby, who cocks one side of her lips before noticing me watching her.

"Large crowd for a patch party," she remarks.

"He's a popular guy."

I maneuver our car into a space near the back of the front driveway. Hayden's out of the back seat before I even get my seatbelt off.

"Hayden!" her mother calls after her.

"She's fine, Shel. Probably just going to look for Red and Walter."

We both exit the car, and meet up at the front of it. Shelby chews away at her bottom lip. The last time she was at a patch party, it was my own, and she left me because of it. Stepping into the door together with our daughter is the start of something new for us as a couple, and as a family. We just needed to take the first step toward our future.

Shelby reaches out, grasping my right hand tightly. I give it a quick squeeze and she smiles at me. The last few weeks gave us the chance to get to know each other all over again. To find out just who we had grown up to be after so many years apart. It was like we were kids again, fumbling through the motions until we got it right. And damn, had we gotten it right. This morning in the laundry room was proof enough of that.

"Should I tell the guys to lock the doors tonight so you don't run away on me again?" I tease.

"We'll see how the night goes," she sasses right back as she jerks my hand, leading me toward the clubhouse door, the music thumping against the exterior of the building.

"Sounds like it's started already."

"Not without the guest of honor."

She stops abruptly, pivoting to look at me, her face covered in confusion.

"Open the door and see for yourself."

She wavers when her hand reaches out for the handle. The door swings wide, and a loud cheer erupts from the inside when we both walk through it.

Every single member of my club, and even a few of the guys from our sister chapters, line the interior of the room under a banner Hayden and I had hung up earlier when Shelby thought we were making a trip to a game store for an expansion pack. Hayden stands next to Lorna with a sign of her own.

Shelby brings her hands to her face when her eyes hit the banner. In big block letters, it reads, *Marry me*, while Hayden's sign reads, *Say yes, Mom!*

I pivot, moving in front of Shelby and slipping my hand into my pocket. She's stunned silent as I kneel in front of her, the crowd going quiet.

"What are you doing?" she whispers.

"Thirteen years ago, I thought I'd lost you. I've spent every one of those years we've been apart trying to figure out a way to find you, to fix what was broken. Then lo and behold, you came barreling back into my life with one of the greatest gifts you could have ever given me."

Shelby lifts her gaze up to look behind us. Reaching up, I grab her hand, holding it in my own.

"I can't promise you that every day is going to be

easy, but I can promise you that even when you want to kill me, I will only love you. When I fuck up, you've got everyone here with us tonight ready to kick my ass back in line. This club is the only family I've ever known until you and Hayden came back into my life. And with my family and yours present, Shelby Jo Dawson, will you do me the honor of marrying me tonight?"

"Tonight?" she chokes out. "We can't get married tonight. We don't have a license or an officiant."

"I can handle the second part of that," Priest yells out from the crowd.

"He's really a priest?" she mutters under her breath. "A biker priest?"

"After everything we've been through, that's the part you question?"

"I guess so," she giggles. "But it won't be legal without the license."

"We'll go to the courthouse tomorrow. I'm not letting another day slip away without you being my wife. I can't risk you running again." I smile up at her. "What do you say, Shel?"

"Say yes already, Mom!" Hayden shouts.

"Yes!"

Revealing the contents of my project, Shelby breaks down into a sobbing mess. The beautiful ring glittering in my hand is the one belonging to her grandmother. I slip it onto her delicate finger and rise, holding her against me.

"How did you get her ring?" she murmurs against my shoulder.

"Lorna. I think she finally likes me."

Hayden comes barreling in between us, hugging us both.

"Don't think I forgot you," I whisper to her. The two of them release me, and Hayden turns to face me. Pulling out a second ring, I hand it to her. Her face pales as she brushes it with her fingers.

"This was the ring I bought for your mom on the night of my patch party. This ring is my commitment to you. No matter what happens, we will always be family."

Curling her hand over the ring, she hugs me tightly. "I love you, Dad."

"And I love you."

"How about we get this show on the road?" Judge bleats out.

Priest shoves his way to the front of the crowd and positions himself between us, while Hayden steps to her mom's side, serving as her maid of honor.

"We are gathered here today to witness the marriage of Shelby Dawson and Wyatt Hayden."

"Wait!" my daughter interjects, stepping between us.

"That's your name? Wyatt Hayden?"

I arch my brow. "Yeah?"

She wrinkles her nose in disgust. "So my name is going to be Hayden Hayden?"

Laughter erupts around the room, but Shelby and I just grin at each other. That's my girl. My girls. My life.

Epilogue

Judge

One Month Later

"FIFTY FUCKING YEARS OLD, GP," I say, gripping a beer bottle in my hand. "That's half a fucking century."

Numbers had never bothered me before. But then, I'd never turned fifty years old before today either. I motion for the waitress to bring another round before turning to watch the girls on the dance floor.

They're all so fucking young. I could be their damn grandfather. That shit is truly depressing.

"Cheer up, old man," Hashtag chuckles, clapping a hand on my shoulder. "Your present will be here soon."

I love my club, and they know I've been struggling. First with Natalie and Kevin, becoming an instant dad to two damaged teenagers. And second, that I'm almost old enough to collect a fucking pension—if I had one.

That's why they'd suggested a new venue. They'd brought me to Sharkey's. This bar is perfect for a guy like me, or so they'd said. It had been once, about fifteen years ago, but now I feel like I should be walking around, handing out condoms and ten-dollar bills.

"Excuse me?"

I turn to see who'd spoken, and take in the tall, slender woman in front of me. Her hair is pulled into a tight little knot at the back of her head, and her glasses are resting on the tip of her nose. She's wearing a business suit, the kind you see in movies with the sport coat and matching skirt. She looks like a librarian, but the girl is stacked, and that's when I realize just what kind of librarian she is.

"Halle-fucking-luja!" I roar, looking around at my boys. "I thought you guys had gotten me something stupid, like a new helmet or a saddlebag for my ride, but this…." I look the librarian up and down with insurmountable approval. "Fucking hell. Happy birthday to me!"

The woman's eyes go wide as she takes a step back. "I beg your pardon?"

"Do you just do the show, or do you provide the after-party too?" I reach for her, wanting to feel her on my lap.

"Judge," GP blurts out from behind me.

"I don't provide any show, sir," she snaps back, her face twisted in anger. "And I don't like what you're insinuating."

Laughing, I take another swig of my beer. "I'm insinuating that I can't wait for you to take off that shirt and show me them gorgeous titties."

"Judge!" GP hollers, but it's too late.

The librarian's hand comes up and slaps the side of my face, hard enough to send my chair sideways.

"I will not be spoken to like that. My name is Grace Halfpenny, and I'm a caseworker for Child Protective Services. I'm looking for a man named Eugene Grant."

Oh shit. I sit up straight in my seat and place the beer gently down on the table. "I'm Eugene."

I ignore the snickers from the guys around the table as Ms. Halfpenny huffs and pulls a stack of papers out of her briefcase, plopping them onto the table in front of me. "Mr. Grant, it has come to my attention that you've been caring for a Kevin and Natalie Tucker without legal right to do so. Those children are wards of the state."

I may have offended her, but I don't like her tone when it comes to those kids. "Those kids are orphans who had nowhere to go. They've had a fucked-up few years, and the last thing they needed was to be separated and shoved into some goddamn foster home."

"Mr. Grant, you don't have the right to make that call."

I stand and move closer, using my size to intimidate her. "I will make whatever call I see fit. Those kids are happy with me, and that's how it's gonna stay."

Her nostrils flare, and I have to remind myself that she's a total bitch, because the look of her pissed off is one of the sexiest things I've ever seen.

"You haven't heard the last of me, Mr. Grant." Turning on her heel, she marches toward the door.

"I liked you better when you were a stripper!" I call out to her back, just trying to piss her off now.

It works. I smirk when my words stop her short, but she doesn't give me the satisfaction of seeing her sweat. Instead, she keeps walking, straight out the door, and hopefully out of my life for good.

Yeah, right.

"Wait," Twat Knot says with a laugh, clearly not getting the brevity of what had just happened. "Your name is Eugene?"

Read more about Judge's story in Dark Guardian.

The Series

Dark Protector

Dark Secret

Dark Guardian

Dark Desires

Dark Destiny

Dark Redemption

Dark Salvation

Dark Seduction

Avelyn Paige is a USA Today and Wall Street Journal bestselling author who writes stories about dirty alpha males and the brave women who love them. She resides in a small town in Indiana with her husband and three fuzzy kids, Jezebel, Cleo, and Asa.

Avelyn spends her days working as a cancer research scientist and her nights sipping moonshine while writing. You can often find her curled up with a good book surrounded by her pets or watching one of her favorite superhero movies for the billionth time. Deadpool is currently her favorite.

Also by Avelyn Paige

The Heaven's Rejects MC Series

Heaven Sent

Angels and Ashes

Sins of the Father

Absolution

Lies and Illusions

The Dirty Bitches MC Series

Dirty Bitches MC #1

Dirty Bitches MC #2

Dirty Bitches MC #3

Other Books by Avelyn Paige

Girl in a Country Song

Cassie's Court

About the Authors

Geri Glenn writes alpha males. She is a USA Today Bestselling Author, best known for writing motorcycle romance, including the Kings of Korruption MC series. She lives in the Thousand Islands with her two young girls, one big dog and one terrier that thinks he's a Doberman,, a hamster and two guinea pigs whose names she can never remember.

Before she began writing contemporary romance, Geri worked at several different occupations. She's been a pharmacy assistant, a 911 dispatcher, and a caregiver in a nursing home. She can say without a doubt though, that her favorite job is the one she does now–writing romance that leaves an impact.

Also By Geri Glenn

The Kings of Korruption MC series.

Ryker

Tease

Daniel

Jase

Reaper

Bosco

Korrupted Novellas:

Corrupted Angels

Reinventing Holly

Other Books by Geri Glenn

Dirty Deeds (Satan's Wrath MC)

Hood Rat

Printed in Great Britain
by Amazon

19330677R00139